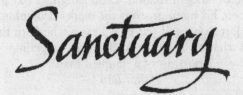

Sanctuary

Acclaim for *Priest*

'Where Bruen really scores is in his intimate explorations of Taylor's character, Galway City and of modern Ireland. Using language like a weapon, his humour stops the reader drowning in rain, Jameson's and self-pity. Less a whodunit than a what-to-do-about-it, this is a compelling portrait of a haunted man'
Guardian

'Bruen's writing is as bleak and spare as Taylor's take on modern Ireland, but you'll end up hooked on this series of home-grown, gritty crime stories as Jack Taylor is on Ireland'
Irish Independent

'Bruen writes tight, urgent powerful prose, his dialogue is harsh and authentic and Jack Taylor has become one of today's most interesting shamuses'
The Times

'Ken Bruen's novel takes us down some dark and mysterious roads where Irish angst meets 21st-century reality in a gripping story of guilt and redemption'
Independent on Sunday

'Tightly structured, compelling . . . You don't want to meet Jack Taylor in person, but if you're a big crime fan, you do want to read every book he features in'
Irish Times

Also by Ken Bruen:

For more information on Ken Bruen and his
books, see his website at www.kenbruen.com

KEN BRUEN

Sanctuary

TRANSWORLD IRELAND

TRANSWORLD IRELAND
61–63 Uxbridge Road, London W5 5SA
A Random House Group Company
www.randomhouse.co.uk

SANCTUARY
A TRANSWORLD IRELAND BOOK: 9781848270183

First published in in Great Britain
in 2008 by Transworld Ireland
Transworld Ireland paperback edition published 2009

Addresses for Random House Group Ltd companies outside the
UK can be found at: www.randomhouse.co.uk
The Random House Group Ltd Reg. No. 954009

Typeset in 11/14½pt Sabon by
Kestrel Data, Exeter, Devon.

10

Penguin Random House is committed to a sustainable future for
our business, our readers and our planet. This book is made from
Forest Stewardship Council® certified paper.

Printed and bound in Great Britain by Clays Ltd, St Ives plc

For Lou Boxer
M. D.
The spirit of David Goodis
Frank Callinan, who restored my faith in lawyers
and
Jay and Lisa Bolick, true renegades
In total admiration

'For my own part, I believe no one on Earth should be so happy as a nun.'

Dame Laurentia McLachlan, Benedictine nun

Part One

'For now at least, all that was to come, and would come in its own delicious time. She would enjoy each minute of what was to come next, let it unfurl as slowly as she liked.'

Cathi Unsworth, *The Singer*

Part One

1

Benediction

Dear Mr Taylor,

Please forgive the formality. We'll progress to a more informal tone. Here is my shopping list – I know you like lists:

Two guards
One nun
One judge
And, alas, one child.

The latter is tragic but inevitable and certainly not negotiable.

But this you already know – the death of a child, I mean.

The list has already begun: see Garda Flynn, deceased two days ago.

Only you will truly comprehend my mission.

You are to be my witness.

I remain, in benediction,

Benedictus

2

Bridge of Sighs

I was standing on the bridge that faces the Spanish Arch in Galway city and the rain was pelting down, drenching me to the core. Despite my all-weather coat, item 8234 of my former Guards issue, and a watchcap pulled down over me forehead, I was soaked. And thinking.

Oh sweet Jesus, if only I could stop thinking.

I should have been in America – even better, down in Mexico, lying on a beach, cold beer on my mind and who knows, maybe a señorita? I certainly had the cash. Yeah, I'd sold my apartment and was sitting on my suitcase, waiting for the cab to the airport. Then the phone had rung.

Even now, I cursed myself for answering.

Ridge, in Irish Ni Iomaire, a female Guard and my partner in hostility and uneasy alliance for years, had been having tests for breast cancer. She was scared, not a thing she ever gave in to, and I was scared too, for her. It's God's own vicious joke, the only woman I managed to keep in my life was gay.

I put the phone to my ear and she had said one word.

'Malignant.'

Is there a more loaded, sinister one in the whole of the language?

I remembered the story about Joyce furiously ripping through a dictionary and Nora Barnacle asking, 'Aren't there enough words in there for you?' And he said, 'Yes, but not the right ones.'

What's the right word for a death sentence?

So I had stayed.

And every single day I was sorry.

Sorry is what I do if not best, certainly most frequently.

They'd removed Ridge's right breast and she was now two months along in recovery.

How does a woman recover from that?

She was out of hospital and recuperating at home, if recuperating means sitting in an armchair, listening to the kind of whining music they give free razor blades with, and drinking.

Yeah, Ridge, drinking. She'd busted my balls for years about my drinking and here she was, sinking into the abyss.

I tried to go round most days to see how she was doing and at first it was a bottle of dry sherry on the mantelpiece, then the bottle was on the coffee table, always getting nearer to reach, and now it was vodka.

First few times, I didn't mention it, especially as she was glaring at me, willing me to go for it.

I didn't.

But finally, a damp cold Monday, not yet noon and there she was, in her dressing gown, the bottle, near empty, perched on the arm of the chair.

'Need to watch that shite, it creeps up on you,' I said to her.

'That's priceless. The last of the real alkies telling me to *watch it*?' She stood up, went to the dresser, took out a pack of cigs, turned and with sheer brazenness lit one and blew the smoke in my direction.

17

Smoking? Another stick she'd beaten me with for so many years.

I was still wearing the patches and hadn't smoked for a long time. Her body language suggested she was ready for war.

Patience has never been one of my strong points. I asked, 'Like me to score you some coke? Then you'd have all my old habits down.'

Her eyes were slits of anger. 'I think I'd have a while to catch up with you, Jack. I mean, how many are in the cemetery because of you?'

It hit me in the stomach like a knife. It was true.

Seeing my reaction, she faltered, tried, 'Sorry, that was uncalled for. I didn't mean . . .'

Was I letting her off the hook? Was I fuck. 'Oh, you meant it, and if you carry on like this, you'll be joining them,' I lashed.

Did I do the childish thing of banging the door on my way out?

You betcha.

I limped down the road, ready to kill some bastard, adjusted my hearing aid, then turned it off. I'd heard enough for one day.

Hearing aid, limp, you're wondering what kind of shape I was in?

Take a wild guess.

The limp was the result of a beating with a hurley, and my hearing had begun to fade in one ear. The specialist asked me, 'Ever get a bang on the head?' Count the ways.

Back on the bridge now.

I could see my beloved swans, so graceful. Sheer poetry to watch them glide on the water. I could just make out the Atlantic Ocean, and but a wish from there was my promised land, America.

The Spanish Arch, of course. Still intact, portal to Long Walk and gateway to the Atlantic. Primarily, it acts as overseer to the old fishing village of the Claddagh and literally, as the line goes, 'Age has not withered its appeal.' The Virgin sits atop the arch, like a forlorn illusion of hope.

I was thinking of the letter I'd received.

It had come about a week before and contained a list of people the writer was going to kill: guards, a nun, a judge and, most frightening of all, a child. A whole series of questions jostled in my mind. How did this lunatic get my address? I'd have to check on that and it worried me, not just the disturbing letter but the psycho knowing where I lived. Should

I get the locks changed? To say these thoughts preyed on my mind is understatement.

I phoned a guy in the Post Office named Sean. I did him a favour a time back and he'd said, 'You ever need anything, give me a call.'

He was friendly, as always, and pre-empted me with 'Jack, anything I can help you with?'

I said, 'I recently changed address and have got a letter from someone I don't know. How would that happen?'

He laughed. 'Easiest thing in the world, mate. We live in a world where information is readily available. Not just your address – if you follow the news you'll see they can find out your bank details nowadays, your credit rating, anything.'

Jesus, that was scary and I told him so.

He made a sound that carried all the implications of *tell me about it*. He said, 'Try working in the Post Office. Lots of people who've had your experience think we are responsible. But Jack, let's lower it a notch, to ease your concern.'

I'd love to hear how he intended to achieve that.

He continued, 'You have, let's face it, a high profile – all that stuff with the tinkers, the Magdalene Laundries, the priest, and just about everybody knows you. How hard would it be to follow you to wherever you live? You're not exactly invisible.'

This was lowering it a notch?

I said, 'Thanks, Sean. I appreciate it.'

'Glad to be of help. Just treat it like junk mail – dump it.'

Right.

I'd sworn I was out of the investigation business, but this was personal, or so the lunatic who wrote it implied. I had some choices.

I could just ignore it, or . . .

That *or* has been the curse of my life.

Earlier that morning, I had checked out the first guard mentioned and sure enough, a Garda Flynn had been killed in a hit and run just over a week ago. The letter-writer could be just using his death to lure me into a sick game, but my instinct told me it wasn't so. Despite Sean's reassurances, this Benedictus knowing where I lived was like an ominous cloud.

I was still staring at the water and a guy passing said, 'Jesus, jump or get off the frigging path.'

He wasn't working with the Samaritans, I guessed.

3

Bless This Humble Abode

I decided I'd better do something about the letter, and the action I thought of filled me with dread.

My best friend, way back in my early days as a young guard, had been Clancy. I got bounced and he went all the way to the top and was now Superintendent. We shared a history. Over the years, my involvement in some cases had made him look bad and he had been determined to even the score. His early friendship with me had become a bitter enmity. He loathed me with a ferocious passion, saw me as a drunk, a loser – you get the picture. And the fact that I'd solved some cases he'd abandoned made it worse.

I was now renting a small place in Dominic Street. It was only temporary, I told myself. When Ridge got back on her feet I'd head for America. It was tiny, just a living room and a bedroom, and cost a fortune, like everything in our new rich city. Someone had cooked a lot of curry in it at one time and the smell still lingered. I had a single bed, ten books, yeah, ten, one sofa, one kettle, and what passed for a shower, behind a cardboard alcove.

Oh, lest I forget, and a portable television, black and white, that flickered constantly, like my bloody life.

Next morning, I was sneezing. I suppose if you stand on a bridge for a few hours in the driving rain, you're not going to be the picture of health.

I dressed in my one suit, a shirt that was more grey than white, a Galway tie and a pair of Timberland boots I'd bought for my trip to America. I'm sure they would have been real useful in Mexico. I had a coffee – black, as I'd forgotten to buy milk. It tasted as bitter as I felt. I took a deep breath and headed out.

At least the rain had stopped and something

that might have been the sun was trying to make an appearance.

It failed.

My building had six apartments and I'd only met one of the neighbours, a very camp gay who liked to play. His name, or so he said, was Albert. 'Or you can call me Hon if you like, big guy.'

How the fuck do I find them or they me? It's like there's a neon sign above my head that reads: 'Gather here, you crazies of all creeds.'

They did.

He was in his very bad late thirties, emaciated to the point of anorexia, always dressed in black and with the worst comb-over I've ever seen.

He was coming out of his apartment and was, of course, dressed in black. On seeing my black suit, he screamed in mock horror, 'Oh my God! One of us will have to change.'

I tried to get past him as quickly as I could, said, 'It's a little late for me to become gay.'

Took him a moment, then he playfully punched my arm.

I loved that.

And he said, 'Oh you, you are wicked.'

Is there a reply to this? I mean, seriously.

He continued, 'Jack. Is it OK to call you Jack? I'm having a little *soirée* on Friday and I'd love you to come. Nothing fancy, just bring yourself and a lot of alcohol or drugs. Just kidding – but do bring drugs.'

I gave him the look. His accent was that new trend, quasi-American and very fucking annoying. I asked, 'Where are you from?'

Paused a second then said, 'Aren't we all citizens of *le monde*, dear heart? But if you must know and you swear never to tell a soul, I'm from Cork.'

I was pretty sure they didn't use *soirée* a whole lot in Cork, but Ireland was changing so fast, maybe they did. I asked, 'And did you play hurling?'

The finest hurlers come from Cork. They are born with a hurley in their fist.

He was not amused. 'Hardly.'

I said, 'Well, here's the deal. In my shitty room there, I've got a hurley and if you ever call me any of those endearments again, I'll give you a real fast lesson in the game.'

He faltered for a moment before recovering. 'You brute, you. Must dash. Don't forget Good Friday.'

I shouted, 'I don't do parties.'

He threw back, 'Never too late to start, even for a man of your senior years.'

Touché.

4

The Blood of the Innocents

The killer was staring at the montage on the wall.

There were photos of two guards, a nun, a judge, a young child and, heading them, a large photo of Jack Taylor. Posted above this in gothic letters was the word **Benediction**. A small table beneath the display held six candles. One had been blown out.

'The first shall be last,' said the killer, addressing the photo of Taylor. The killer had left out that little detail from the letter, wanted it to be a surprise.

'Sanctus.'

Kill Taylor.

The killer took a long carving knife from

the table and began to cut a deep wedge along the right arm. The pain was a moment in arriving and when it did, the killer let out a deep *aah* of agonized pleasure, whispered, 'The blood of the innocents.'

5

Merton Mania

I hadn't phoned ahead for an appointment with Superintendent Clancy – he'd have blown me off so I was going cold. I didn't have far to go. The Guards station was at the top of Dominic Street, and a sign across from it, mounted over the river, proclaimed, 'Call the Samaritans first!'

And what?

If they didn't help, you could jump in the river?

The station was relatively quiet, and thank Christ, the young guard behind the counter didn't know me. I asked if I might see the super. He inquired as to the nature of my business and asked for my name. I gave that then said, 'Personal.'

He told me to take a seat and picked up the phone.

His face changed as he listened and I knew he was getting an earful on who I was. He summoned me and now he'd a hard edge. 'He's in a meeting. Won't be free for at least two hours.'

I said I'd wait.

I'd been expecting this shite and had brought along a book, *The Secular Journal of Thomas Merton.*

Merton and a pint had been my staple diet for years until I lost faith in him and the pints lost faith in me. Fair trade off, I guess. Now I was trying to reconnect with him. I cracked open the book and hit on this:

'I read William Saroyan when I was too tired to read the hard stuff.'

Jesus, I was too tired for the hard stuff.

I became engrossed in Merton's account of Harlem and almost didn't feel the three hours go by.

Almost.

The station was getting busy, a line of non-nationals seeking driving licences, passports, help. They were cowed and defeated in their demeanour.

Welcome to the land of a thousand welcomes.

A drunk was dragged in by two burly cops, shouting, 'Kerry will win the All Ireland!' As they tried to drag him to the cells, he spotted me, screamed, 'I know you. You're a drunk.'

I didn't answer.

One of the guards gave him a wallop on the side of the head and he shut up. The non-nationals pretended not to see it; they were learning the game.

Finally, the young guard called me, said, 'He'll see you now.' Then added with a smirk, 'Sorry to have kept you waiting.'

Right.

I was buzzed through to Clancy's office. It was even larger than I remembered and alight with awards, citations, honours. He was dressed in his full regalia, the dress blues, the stripes. He'd put on a ton of weight, he looked like a fat Buddha in a uniform, without the serenity. On his massive desk was a sheaf of files and a framed photo of him, his wife, I presume and a young boy. There was a hard chair in front of the desk and I looked at it.

'Don't bother, you won't be here long enough to warm yer arse,' he said.

'And good to see you too, Super.'

He snapped, 'Boyo, don't try any of your lip, I'll have you out of here in jig time. I thought you'd fucked off to America and we were finally rid of you.'

I gave him my best smile. I have terrific teeth, cost me a bundle after a guy removed my old ones with an iron bar. I said, 'I got side-tracked.'

He leaned back in his chair, gave me his full inspection, then said, 'A hearing aid! Doesn't seem to have improved your ability to listen much. What do you want? And make it brief.'

I told him about the letter, showed it to him.

He laughed, not out of warmth or humour, asked, 'You write this yourself, Taylor?'

I counted to ten, then said, 'Garda Flynn was killed, just like it says there.'

He threw the letter back at me. 'An unfortunate hit and run. Is this what you've wasted my time for?'

I tried to remember the time when we'd been friends, but it was too long ago. I asked, 'Won't you at least check it out?'

He stood up. Despite his weight, he was

still imposing. Oozing hostility, he said, 'We have serious business to attend to, not this nonsense. Take my advice, Taylor. Get the fuck to America or wherever, there's nothing for you in this town, in my town.'

I stood up. 'And if there's another death, what then?'

He shook his head. 'Go on, get out of here. Have a drink or something, it's all you're fit for.'

At the door I said, 'God bless you.'

He indicated my book, said, 'It's that rubbish that has you the nobody you are.'

6

Forgive Us Our Trespasses

Judge M. Healy was the very opposite of a so-called 'hanging judge'.

He went so far in the other direction that it had become a running joke. Defence lawyers loved him, and the prosecution loathed and despised him. His motivation was one: notoriety, and two: he'd been a defence lawyer and had been slapped down so often, he was out to make his mark another way.

It got him the headlines he craved and inflated his ego. In the previous six months, he'd had before him:

A violent rapist. Sentence: two years suspended.

A paedophile priest. Sentence: counselling.

A wife beater. Sentence: Six months' community service.

A drunk driver who killed a young woman: Sentence: rehab.

Outrage, of course, but short-lived and soon forgotten.

Removing a judge in Ireland is like trying to stop the Galway rain. Plus, he was a huge supporter of the government and, with elections due, he was secure.

And smug with it.

Very.

He'd reply, when challenged, 'The jails are overcrowded. I'm giving these people a second chance.'

And it never cost him a moment's sleep.

He kept a luxury apartment in the city centre and used it to entertain the growing number of women who sought his *expertise*. Life was good and he knew it was only a matter of time till he got appointed to the supreme court.

That Friday evening, he finished court early. He was the judge, he could finish whenever he wished. He was anticipating an evening of fine food, some vintage cognac, a call from the government chief whip, and a young lady to blow his trumpet later.

He reached the apartment feeling as if he ruled the world, and rubbed his stomach at what the evening promised. He poured himself a cognac, swirled it round in the glass and let out a deep *aah* of contentment. When the brandy had warmed his stomach, he went into the bedroom to change into something loose and comfortable.

He nearly dropped his snifter when he saw the noose dangling in the middle of the room, and a voice said, 'You get to be the hanging judge after all.'

7

Zen Mode

I was having a coffee in the Eyre Square Centre, listening to the various conversations round me. The main topic was the poisoning of the water system. Nearly a quarter of the town had been to the hospital with diarrhoea and vomiting, and some of the schools had been closed. The bug lasted up to two weeks and finally the powers that be had announced that the water was contaminated and instructed us not to drink it.

I thought, *Now they tell us?*

They suspected a parasite in the water. Tests were being carried out and meanwhile, they suggested, we should boil all water or drink bottled water.

In other words, they hadn't a clue and were covering their arses.

The supermarkets had run out of supplies and were madly scrambling to get bottled water brought in from nearby towns.

I had no idea how it was I'd escaped. Being sober, of course, I wasn't dehydrated and so had no need of water as such.

A shadow fell across me and I looked up to see Stewart, my former drug-dealer, who'd spent six years in jail. I'd helped solve the murder of his sister and he felt indebted. He'd become a Zen student and tried to enlist me.

Right.

Prison had given him a hard edge but he covered it with the Zen stuff. His eyes had a granite sheen that told otherwise. I don't know if we were friends but we were connected.

He said, 'Mr Taylor, might I join you?'

I indicated the empty chair and he sat in one fluid motion. He was wearing a very expensive blazer, knitted tie, blinding white shirt and grey slacks, and looked prosperous. I had no idea what he did now, but it clearly paid well. I asked if he'd like anything and he quoted, '"He who is satisfied with his lot is rich."'

I sighed. 'I'll take that as no.'

He was in his early thirties, and yet had the air of someone much older. Prison ages you in ways that aren't always visible.

I asked, 'How come you're not involved with someone? Married, even?'

This amused him, as did most things I said. He answered, '"One must know oneself before one can relate."'

Jesus.

I tried again. 'You strike me as a bloke who knows himself pretty damn well.'

'Outward appearance, Jack, and if I may be so forward, always your downfall. I seek to find the inner core.'

I'd had enough of this horseshite, said, 'Any chance you'll talk like a normal person?'

He was further amused and asked, 'How is your friend, the Ban Garda? Ridge.'

I told him she was drinking and he said, 'Perhaps your own . . . er . . . life experience may be of help?'

My expression answered that for him.

He leaned in close. 'I've some news that may either be of some comfort or deep distress, and I meditated long and hard before deciding to share it with you.'

I said, 'Stewart, the only thing that would

really surprise me any more is good news, though I'm not sure I'd recognize it.'

Ignoring my flippancy, he said, 'This is truly life-altering news and I want you to be sure you can handle it.' He stared at me, gauging how well or unwell I was, then asked, 'When the little girl went out the window, Jack, what were you doing?'

It was the central tragedy of my life. I'd been minding my best friend's little girl, lost focus and she went out the window. My life effectively ended then, as did the lives of her parents, Jeff and Cathy. Jeff had become a street person and Cathy disappeared. She might have been the one who shot my surrogate son, Cody.

Stewart said, 'I regret having to resurrect such pain for you, Jack, but did you by any chance doze off when you were looking after her?'

It was possible, but I was getting agitated and shouted, 'What the fuck does it matter? I wasn't paying attention, and Sere—'

I couldn't say her name, went with 'The little one went out the window. What are you implying?'

He took his time, then said, 'What if someone else pushed her out the window?'

I was stunned, then raging. I nearly went for him, snarled, 'Are you fucking mad? It was my fault. I live with it every day and now you trot out this nonsense.'

He put his hand on my arm but I shrugged it off.

He said, 'Jack, you're my friend. Why would I deliberately upset you?'

Jesus, I could feel tears in my eyes.

I'd been doing penance for so long, tears were no longer part of the daily trip. I asked, 'What is this about?'

He exhaled a long breath, then said, 'One of my ex-clients was in rehab and she shared a room with a woman. You know how total honesty and making amends, all that good karma, is part of the whole gig? This woman said she pushed her own child out the window and let someone else take the rap.'

It was like being hit by a truck. I stammered, 'Cathy?'

He nodded.

I couldn't take it in.

'That's impossible.'

His voice quiet, he ventured, 'Wasn't that time exceptionally hot? A heatwave, if I recall. And you were coming off a bad case. Isn't it possible you nodded off for five minutes?'

'Christ almighty.' All these years of such agony, guilt – for nothing? 'Why? Why would she do such a thing? She adored that child.'

He took his time, then said, 'The little girl had Down syndrome. Her mother felt she'd be better off out of a world that would only hurt and ridicule such a child. It's not uncommon.'

I was reeling, spat, 'She threatened to kill me. She let her husband go down the toilet, and all the time she was the one. The fucking bitch, how could she do that?'

He said, 'Denial is a very powerful tool, Jack, and Cathy used to be a junkie, right?'

I said, 'I'll fucking kill her.' I meant it. I was nearly blind from tears and rage.

He waited, then said, 'Don't you think she does that to herself, every single day?'

My whole body began to shake, from anger, hurt, confusion and the terrible waste and loss.

Stewart reached in his suit jacket, took out a small envelope and slid it across the table. 'Take one of these babies, you won't be hurting. No more than two a day.'

I wanted to say, *Shove your fecking pills*. But I'm an alky and thus, as an addict, open to anything mind-altering. The last years of my drinking had been about numbness. I was no longer seeking joy or fun. I was drinking, as Exley said, to 'Simply dim the lights'. Fred Exley's book *A Fan's Notes* was nigh essential reading for a drinker, and though the words are somewhat different in the book, that's what he meant. The lights had been glaring for years and, alas, not blinding me but allowing me to see all too clearly. There was no greater curse.

I took a pill out. It was large and black and I raised my eyebrows.

'Black beauties,' he said simply.

I had to ask, 'And are they beauties?'

He gave a tight smile, no warmth. It was a long time since Stewart did warmth; the closest he ever came was his odd friendship with me. Music was playing over the speakers and Snow Patrol came on with 'Set The Fire To The Third Bar'. Hell of a title and hell of a song.

Stewart asked, 'You'll be returning to your day job, I suppose?'

Investigating.

I said, 'Soon as Ridge gets in shape, I'm outa here.'

Like any ex-con, his eyes were continually darting round, checking the exits, the people, gauging the threat. I realized how sad but true

47

it was that you could leave prison but it would never leave you.

He said, 'If you need any help, I'm available. And as you know, I know everyone, in some capacity.'

So I showed him the list and, unlike Clancy, he didn't dismiss it, said, 'A judge killed himself yesterday.' He filled me in on the details and then added, 'Around his neck was a placard with the block letters I HAVE TRESPASSED.'

Christ on a bike.

I said, 'That's the same language as in the letter.'

He studied the list, then said, 'Any idea who it might be?'

I shook my head.

'Lemme root around.'

'You'll want paying?' I asked.

That icy smile again. 'Course.'

Then before I could say anything, he said, 'Let me share my Zen learning with you.'

Ah fuck.

I said, 'I'd rather pay you in, like, cash.'

He was standing now, said, 'Cash doesn't last. I think you and me both know that.'

8

Anglo-Irish

I'd just approached the entrance to my flat when a BMW pulled up, like in the movies or a bad novel, with a screech of brakes. The door opened and what Mickey Spillane would call a *bruiser* got out. He was one of the largest men I've ever seen, and remember, I'd trained as a young guard with the men from the Midlands and they don't come much bigger. This guy was.

He didn't quite have cauliflower ears but it was a close call. Scar tissue round his eyes testified to his time as a boxer. He moved right up to me, said, 'Taylor, someone wants to meet you.'

He was wearing an expensive suit but it

didn't conceal his bulk; he was used to his sheer size doing his work for him. I was in a pretty shitty frame of mind, close to real meltdown, and this fuck, with his tone, got me in all the wrong ways. I asked, 'And who might that be?'

He gave a condescending smile, making me like him even less, if possible, and sneered, 'All in good time, bud. Get in the car.'

Bud?

He was right in my face and I could smell aniseed on his breath, very strong and nauseating. I asked, 'And if I don't?'

He loved that, like he'd been hoping I'd take that route. He jabbed a fat finger in my chest and said, 'Then I'll put you in.'

I kneed him in the balls, hard, and as he doubled over, I caught him by his expensive lapel and said, 'Tell your boss to make an appointment and get some decent help.'

I gave him a light slap on the face, added, 'And don't call me bud.'

I let him slump to the ground and went inside feeling a whole lot better. My gay neighbour was waiting, wringing his hands, looking scared. I was in no mood for theatrics, snapped, 'What?'

He was shaking as he handed me a leaflet and asked, 'Have you seen this?'

'What the fuck is it now?'

I took the leaflet, read:

> BUGGER BOYS ARE A VIRUS
> LEAVE WHILE YOU STILL CAN
> THIS IS NOT A WARNING
> IT'S A PROMISE.
>
> O. F. R. L.

I read it twice. 'What do the initials stand for?'

He looked at me in astonishment. 'You don't know?'

Jesus.

'If I bloody knew, would I be asking?' My meltdown was back.

He wrung his hands some more and said, 'Organization For Right Living.'

I thought, *Just what the town needs. The water is poisoned and here are a bunch of crazies with their own brand of poison.*

I said, 'Fucking head cases. Chuck it in the bin.'

Still shaking, he said, 'They've been beating up gay people outside clubs.'

Bollocks. 'People get walloped outside clubs all the time, it's part of the entertainment. How do you even know it's them?'

He stood back, his outrage overcoming his fear, and said, 'Because they have a hot iron and brand those letters on your hand.'

I'd had enough. 'So stay home or call the cops.'

He spat, 'The cops, right, they would just love to defend homosexuals. In Catholic Ireland, they're probably part of the organization.'

As I put the key in my door I said, 'You run across them, give me a shout.'

I was inside, shutting the door when he called, 'And who exactly is it you'd help, them or me?'

I turned the radio on to drown him out.

My mind was in tatters. The shattering thought that I wasn't responsible for the death of Serena May was too much to take in. All those years of guilt and the subsequent fallout because of it.

Jesus wept.

Here's the horrendous deal: an alcoholic can stay dry under the most trying circumstances. You'll hear people wonder that he didn't drink at the wedding/funeral when everybody expected him to.

An alkie can stumble drinkless through all these minefields, and then one tiny incident, like a shoelace snapping or a carton of milk spilling, and wallop, he's off on the most almighty binge.

Ordinary people can't understand this and even the alkie is baffled.

I was in this zone now.

I was, as it were, nigh exonerated of the ferocious burden that had marked and dogged my every waking moment, and now, free in a sense, I wanted to drink more than during all the days of darkness. I must have been grappling with all of this for hours till, exhausted, I dozed off.

The phone pulled me from my sleep. My neck was stiff from lolling in the armchair. I grabbed the phone, muttering, 'Better be fucking good.'

Said, 'Yeah?'

'Mr Taylor?'

Uh-oh. Mister. Not a promising start. I snarled, 'So?'

An intake of breath, then a very cultured voice, what we call the West Brit one, went, 'Mr Taylor, firstly let me apologize for my man's heavy-handed tactics, he has received a stern reprimand . . .' An amused chuckle, then he continued, 'But I think it was mild in comparison to your own – shall we say, response. The poor chap is still bent over.'

I wanted a drink, a large one, and now. 'I get it, you're the prick who wants to see me. Didn't you ever consider asking politely? And how did you get my address?'

I'd been worried about the psycho who sent the letter knowing where I lived, and now this guy knew too – the thug had been waiting outside my home.

I asked, more forcibly, 'How do you know where I live?'

A pause, then he said, 'Mr Taylor, I know a lot of influential people and trust me, they know where everybody is located, and I mean everybody. And in truth, you are not the hardest man in the city to find.'

Another pause as he let me digest this.

He cleared his throat. 'I deeply regret the fumbled attempt to make contact with you, but I will compensate you adequately.'

I cut him off. 'Who the hell are you? And what's the urgency in meeting me? And OK, my address, you asked around – but how did you get my phone number?'

He gave a slight sigh as if I was slow. 'I had my man spread around a few euro in your usual haunts and sure enough, a man – a friend of yours, I suppose – gave it up for twenty. Tut tut, Jack. Select your friends more carefully, or at least the ones you give your number to.'

I was very angry. It was that easy to get my number? I felt I already had his. A wanker with money and an over-developed sense of his own importance. He said, 'Allow me to introduce myself.'

Only much later did I realize how similar to The Stones' opening line of 'Sympathy For The Devil' this sounded.

'I'm Anthony Bradford-Hemple. No doubt you are familiar with the name?'

I'd like to say he uttered this with smugness or conceit, but no, it was simply a matter of fact. The whole world knew him; his name was a given.

I did know it.

Anglo-Irish landowners, they owned large tracts of land outside Oranmore and were famous for their stables, but like many of these families, the sheer upkeep of their large estates, the cost of heating their old houses, had made them tighten their belts. An Irish irony: as the ordinary people got wealthy from our new prosperity, these old relics of affluent history were feeling, as they'd term it themselves, *the pinch.*

I hadn't actually heard a dicky bird about them in a long time as they'd gone off the radar. And OK, I didn't exactly move in circles where their names came up much.

You're an ex-guard with a limp, a hearing aid and a drink problem, the goings-on of the rich and famous aren't your top priority. I wasn't likely to be applying for a subscription to *Hello!* magazine, but was I going to admit to knowing him?

Was I fuck.

I said, 'That name doesn't mean dick to me, fellah.'

A slight intake of breath as he digested the insult, then, 'Well, Mr Taylor, they did warn me that you had a caustic tongue, but regardless, I'd like to engage your services.'

I let him hear me sigh, went, 'Let's hear it.'

He cleared his throat and I wondered if he wore a cravat – they nearly always did. He said, 'My only daughter Jennifer was sixteen a few weeks back and, naturally, I got her a pony.'

Naturally.

His voice shook. 'The pony was stolen and I received its tail in the mail, with a note saying that if I didn't pay fifty thousand euros, Jennifer would be next.'

Jesus.

I've had swans, dogs feature in my battered history, and now ponies. What was I? The alky version of Ace Ventura?

He added, 'The police claim they are working on it, but so far, nothing, You have a reputation for getting results when the official channels fail. Will you help me? Please, Mr Taylor, I'll reward you handsomely. My wife died some years ago and Jennifer is all I have.'

Then I had a thought. I wanted to get Ridge back on track and I knew she loved horses, so I said, 'Give me your address and I'll have my associate contact you.'

He wasn't wild about that, but I assured him she'd only be taking notes and I'd be handling the case personally.

He ended with, 'You won't regret this, Mr Taylor.'

I already did.

9

The White Feather

I readied myself for Ridge, not sure how she was going to receive my proposal that she join my *firm*. Yeah, I know how that sounds – my one and only *employee* had been my surrogate son, Cody, and as the Americans say, 'he took a bullet for me' . . . literally, and he was now where just about everyone who had contact with me was.

Buried.

I was still reeling from the revelation that I wasn't responsible for Serena May's death. It had been the focal point of my whole existence these past years. The guilt, the nightmares – and wallop, I didn't do it.

I could now finally think about that gorgeous

child, the button nose, the cherubic face, and not be devastated. Christ, I loved her more than mere alcohol would allow, and worse, she loved me too. I made her laugh and she had such a wondrous heart-warming one, you could believe in angels. And even as I thought this, the church bell from the Claddagh began to toll. The old people say, 'When you hear a bell ring, it's an angel getting her wings.' Mind you, the old folk believe all kinds of weird shite. Still, I kind of liked the notion, though I knew fuck all about angels. Demons and devils were my crew.

Another pishog, that's Irish for a story that is not only untrue but superstitious too, is that if you find a white feather, an angel is close by.

Bollocks . . . right?

And how it goes, the line from Kristofferson's song came unbidden, about a bell in loneliness being rung.

I turned on the radio as I dressed, and the nurses were on strike, the swans were dying from some mysterious virus, and the water, always the water these days. Dentists were advertising that they only used bottled water when you rinsed and the priests were using bottled water in the fonts. I don't know about holy water but it sure was expensive. The poor and the needy were being given free bottled water with their state hand-out. The council, as we headed into Lent, were now saying that it would be September before the water could be declared safe. And we were going to believe them then?

The pubs were swearing that their ice was made from bottled water. The supermarkets were panic-buying all of the supplies of bottled water. A little girl had asked, if you go swimming, will the sea be boiled first?

Most important of all, for the ones who ruled the city, was the fear of tourists staying away, and already counties like Donegal were trading on our misfortune, advertising COME TO WHERE THE WATER IS SAFE.

I had boiled up a stash of water and put it in plastic bottles.

A new traffic superintendent, who'd been lecturing us for the whole month about the evils of drink-driving and how he'd bring the wrath of God on anyone caught, was arrested by a young rookie, so drunk he could hardly get into his car. Did he get the wrath of God? He got a golden handshake of nigh on a quarter of a million and his pension of forty thousand euro was untouchable.

Some wrath, eh?

And to cap it all, as the elections approached, the prime minister was being accused by his former driver of bringing money in plastic bags to Manchester. He seemed highly indignant – more about the plastic bags than the money.

I drained the last of my coffee and was about to go when Philip Fogarty and Anna Lardi came on with the haunting 'Lullaby For The Nameless'. It is as gut-wrenching as the title suggests. I felt a jolt in my heart and an aching for a very large Jameson. The booze had inched a degree nearer.

I was wearing a sweatshirt that had a faded but legible logo that proclaimed: SUSPICIOUS CIRCUMSTANCES. Perfect for a PI in disguise.

Fogarty had another killer with 'Inhumane', but that was too close to the bone for me. I got the hell out of there. I adjusted my hearing aid to low, and in my newish 501s felt my limp wasn't too noticeable.

The weather had been unseasonably sunny and I turned my face up to the sun, felt the early-morning heat. I turned right by the fire station and headed out towards the tech college. A business school was situated next to the park there and a cluster of students were outside, smoking. Since the smoking ban had come into effect, more young people than ever had taken up the habit and as I passed, I heard them chatter. Not one of them was Irish. One tenth of the population was now non-national and the number was increasing. If they were happy to be in our shiny new rich country, they were hiding it well. They scowled at me as I passed, but maybe it was because I seemed . . . admit it . . . old. As I turned into Grattan Road, I could see the beach, the ocean, and I let it soothe me as it always did.

A man was sitting on a bench. He had a collie on a leash, straining to get free and run on the beach. He was wearing a heavy black-leather jacket. He looked up and smiled, revealing huge gaps in his teeth. 'Jack Taylor, I heard you were in the madhouse.'

Nice greeting.

I could have said the country was one open-air asylum, but went with 'How've you been?'

This is the Irish version of 'I've no idea what your name is.'

And I didn't.

He drew up a huge amount of phlegm from his heaving chest then spat to the side and said, 'I'm well fucked. They say I have a tumour on me lungs and need treatment.'

He needed some lessons in manners too, but I kept that to meself, asked, 'When do you begin?'

He reined in the dog, pulling harshly on the lead and cutting off the poor thing's air, looked at me as if I was stupid, went, 'Begin what?'

I wanted to get the hell away from him, sighed. 'The treatment.'

He gave a very nasty laugh. 'Don't be fucking dense, Taylor. You let them butchers at you, you're already buried.'

Before I could venture an opinion, he pointed to the beach. 'See that family, down near the water?'

A black family, their laughter and joy carrying on the Galway breeze. They looked happy and it eased the darkness this guy was breathing.

He said, 'Niggers, stealing our country right from under us. Try getting a white doctor in the hospital.' He let out a sneering laugh which caused another upshot of spit. '. . . Good fucking luck. All the white doctors have legged it to Dublin, and you know, if I let Brandy here loose to run on the beach like she loves, them bastards would think, dinner.'

Disgusted, I turned to go. I muttered, 'Take care.'

He patted his jacket. 'I'm carrying a hatchet, that's all the care I need.'

You could ask what made him so nuts, so full of hatred. All I can say is: 'the new Ireland'.

No matter how hostile Ridge was going to be, she'd be a ray of sunshine compared to him. There's a song titled 'Home Is Where The Hatred Is'.

I thanked Christ I couldn't remember the words.

10

Ice

I looked round. Not a feather in sight, not even a black one.

As I turned into Grattan Park, I knew I was only about five minutes from Ridge's house and I slowed my pace, reluctant to face the scene I expected, to see her fucked and bedraggled from booze. And saw an off-licence beckoning. It was a new one, but then, in my years of dryness God only knew how many had opened up. The water might be poisoned, but by Jesus, we weren't letting the virus affect our drinking habits.

Sure enough, a sign in the window proclaimed, 'Our ice cubes are made by Alto.'

So, a company had sprung up to meet the

need for purified ice? When I was a child, ice was something you might see on Christmas Eve.

I went in, saw the bottles of tequila on display – another trend I'd missed. Shots of tequila being de rigueur for the young, wealthy kids who hit the clubs . . . 'De rigueur' – took me years to find a way to use that, never mind figure out what the hell it meant.

On the wall was a poster advertising Philip Fogarty and Anna Lardi in concert. I clocked the rows of cigarettes and had a pang for another addiction denied. I grabbed a bottle of Grey Goose, because it came with a free T-shirt and I figured Ridge hadn't been doing a whole lot of laundry.

The kid at the register was non-national. Rang up my bottle and said, 'That be twenty-eight euro.'

Me thinking, *That be fucking exorbitant.*

He put the bottle and the T-shirt in a bag that screamed, *off-licence.*

I paid him. He never said 'thank you' or anything related to it and I was about to say something when I heard, 'Taylor, back on the drink?'

Turned to see Father Malachy, my nemesis,

an adversary for so many years and, worse, a friend of my late mother.

We might actually have become, if not friends, allies of an uneasy kind when he enlisted my help for a case. A priest had been murdered and Malachy, desperate, had turned to me for help. I did conclude it and, albeit a terrible conclusion, the case had been solved. Not my finest hour. He didn't know the full details, only that I'd helped him. Thus you'd expect, if not gratitude, at least a certain appreciation.

But no, it made us more combative than ever.

He reeked of nicotine, his black priest's jacket was littered with dandruff and ash, his teeth brown from his addiction.

I said, 'Good to see you, Father.'

It wasn't.

He eyed my purchase, said, 'You couldn't stay off it, could you?'

The temptation to kick the living shite out of him was as compelling as ever. Instead, I thought of the letter I'd received and asked, 'What do you know about benediction?'

He was taken aback, silent for a moment.

'Why? What do you want to know?'

I had him intrigued and pushed, 'I got a letter, a threatening one, with the signature "Benedictus".'

He shrugged. 'Benediction is a blessing, but in your case can only be a curse.' And he moved past me, heading for the cartons of cut-price cigarettes.

I resisted the temptation to kick him in the arse.

It took some doing.

I said, 'See you soon.'

Without even turning round, he spat, 'Not if God is good.' Nice ecclesiastical parting remark.

I got outside, rage rampant in my head, and in an effort to calm down recalled an incident a few weeks back with Stewart.

I'd been in some state, with Ridge in the hospital, the booze calling and regrets about my aborted getaway to America swirling in my head, and I'd run into Stewart. He'd taken one look at my face and suggested we go back to his place and, like, chill.

Chill! The way these young Irish talk.

But I'd gone. He'd given me a Xanax and whoa . . . jig time, I was enveloped in if not the cloud of unknowing, certainly the mellow shroud of laid-back ease.

I'd said, 'Jesus, that is one fucking great pill.'

He'd smiled, said, 'Read John Straley, see how long it lasts.'

Who? I didn't care.

Then Stewart did an odd thing. OK, everything the guy did was odd, but he came to where I was stretched out on the sofa and presented me with a long leather case.

I asked, not caring, 'And this is?'

He gestured for me to open it.

Inside were seven beautiful knives, exquisitely made, like the Gurkhas use.

I gazed at them in total admiration, whistled, 'Wow.'

He gave that enigmatic smile, like *wow* was as much as he could expect from me, explained, 'Kabuki knives. You'll notice there are seven, for each stage of my life.'

The Xanax had kicked in big time and I could listen to whatever Zen bullshit he wanted to pedal. I muttered, 'And which number are you on now?'

He lifted one out gently, with more care than if it was a baby. 'The sixth, I term it . . . I'll explain when you are a little further along the road to enlightenment.'

I was cool, or indeed *chill* enough to ask, 'So, these knives, they tell you what?'

He leaned right into my face, said in a stone tone, 'What do they tell you, Jack?'

Even with the pill, I was ready to rumble, *You know, they tell me fuck all. And mainly they tell me, you need to get out more.*

I said, 'They're impressive. What are they meant to be – the Seven Samurai?'

He stared at them. 'They are for the seven levels of evil. Each one removes another layer of the ills that bedevil our world.'

I should have paid more attention to what he was telling me, and later I'd learn exactly what the levels of evil were, but then they were just knives – impressive but, you know, just fucking blades. I'd seen enough of them and was tempted to say, *A Stanley knife is just as useful.* But the Xanax whispered, *Who cares?*

He stood back, considered me, then said, 'Stand up.'

Was he kidding? I'd eat him for breakfast. But what the hell, he wanted to take a shot at me. I was up for it. He moved right into me, his arms hanging by his sides, palms outwards in the classic show of non aggression, said, 'Hit me.'

I laughed. Long time since I'd had cause and I don't suppose the medication hindered my mood either. I scoffed, 'You're fucking kidding.'

He didn't move, his face set in a serious mode. 'I mean it, Jack. Hit me with all you've got.'

I shook my head. 'Stewart, I like you. You piss me off with all the Zen bollocks. But hit you? I don't think so.'

He never moved, said, 'You've got a limp, a hearing aid, and a dead child to your credit.'

I swung with all my might and . . . where'd he go? I hit air.

He was standing to my right, smiled, asked, 'That your best, Jack? Losing your sight too?'

I lashed out with me foot and missed again. Where was he getting this speed from? For five more minutes, I tried in vain. Zip, nada, couldn't touch him.

He said, 'With Zen and a few other Eastern disciplines, I've learned how to be at one.'

I was breathing hard and seriously pissed. 'Yeah, did you learn how to hit, though?'

And I was flat on my back, a throbbing in my throat where he'd taken me with the side of his left hand.

Guess that answered that.

When I got my wind back, I said, 'You're good. What's your point?'

He did a flexing routine, said, 'As well as Zen, I can teach you some moves that will make you less vulnerable.'

I said I'd think about it. When I was leaving, he was standing at the door. I said, 'Oh shit, forgot me jacket.' He turned and I rabbit-punched him. As he went down hard I said, 'It ain't Zen but it sure is effective.'

I'd swear, though he had to be hurting, he was smiling. Mad bastard.

I wasn't sure why I was replaying this unless somewhere in my mind I expected Ridge to attack me. One way or another, she always did.

I'd reached her house. Took a deep breath and rang the bell.

11

Sweet Sobriety

Ridge surprised me all right. She was sober, dressed in clean clothes, her eyes clear, and was holding a book. I nearly smiled. Books had brought me through so many hangovers, not that I could read them then, but they were a lifeline to some semblance of sanity.

I said, 'You look good.'

She waved me in, asked if I'd like some coffee. While she went to make it, I took a look at the book she'd put aside. *Something to Hide.*

Got that right, I thought.

It was by Penny Perrick, an account of the life of Sheila Wingfield, Viscountess Powerscourt. Talk about perfect timing. I was about to ask her to investigate a case involving the West Brits or Anglo-Irish or whatever the fuck you called them and here she was, reading about them. Sometimes you get lucky. I don't, but this was definitely a help.

She came back with two mugs of coffee. 'Biscuits?'

I said, 'I don't do sweet.'

She nodded, knowing the truth of that.

'Interesting reading,' I said.

Ridge sat, sipped at her coffee, her usual antagonism not on display. Least not yet. She said, 'It's odd, I'm as Irish as it gets, reared in the Irish language and everything nationalistic, and not exactly in the lap of luxury, and yet I find a resonance with her.'

I didn't know zip about the woman so I asked, 'Why?'

I really wanted to say I'd never seen Ridge with a book in all the time I'd known her and she had been more than dismissive of my reading. She put her coffee aside.

'She was an Anglo-Jewish heiress, a poet, and the wife of the very last of the Powerscourts. She was racked by drink, drugs and illness, in conflict with the tradition she was supposed to maintain. She never really fitted into any of the worlds she tried to live in.'

I could see the parallels. Ridge was a female guard in a force that worshipped macho bullshit, and worse, she was gay. A young woman, now she was threatened by cancer and could do little but wait.

I nodded in what I hoped was sympathetic understanding. 'Maybe I'll read it.'

She said, 'I doubt it.'

I wanted to ask her how she'd pulled herself together but she got there before me.

'You're wondering how come I'm still not sucking on a bottle?'

Jesus. Not the way I'd have phrased it, but yeah, the content was right.

'I'm just glad to see you, OK.'

She laughed. 'Good old Jack, evasive as ever.'

Old?

She added, 'Actually, it was you who helped me stop whining and drinking.'

'What did I do?'

She looked right at me. 'I've seen you stupefied by drink so many times, drowning in self-pity, hitting out at everyone, and I asked myself, do I really want to be like that?'

The lash was back. I should have known it wouldn't last. I wanted to say, *So happy to have provided you with the motivation.*

Instead I tried to bite down my anger, asked, 'Would you like a job? You know, till you get back on the force?'

I told her about the phone call from Anthony Bradford-Hemple, the young girl's missing pony and the threats. Instead of ridiculing me, she seemed delighted. She got her notebook, took down the details, said she'd go out there today.

I was surprised. I'd expected her to be insulted, offended, and to tell me to stick it. I asked, 'You don't mind working for me?'

She stood, all energy now, said, 'I'm not working for you, I'm helping you out. Or were you going to put me on a salary?'

Christ, she was right back to her old self.

'The guy is loaded and will pay well,' I told her.

She was already grabbing a coat, anxious to get going. 'I'm not doing it for money,' she said.

I couldn't resist the crack, said, 'Very noble of you.'

As she opened the door to send me on my way she added, 'And I'm certainly not doing it for you.'

12

Dark Preparation

Benedictus was naked, staring in a full-length mirror, and with the left hand traced the tattoo along the stomach.

Then, taking a very sharp knife, began to remove the tattoo. The pain was almost unbearable, and yet exquisite agony.

Benedictus began to envision how the killing of the nun would play out – lure her into a trap, then very slowly strangle the wretch to all damnation.

13

All That Shines

I was in Busker Brown's, a pub just off Quay Street. They have a jazz morning on Sundays and it is always packed. Today, though, a weekday, it was quiet. They do a very fine Colombian roast – no, not dope, coffee – and I savoured the sheer bite of it as I opened the paper, the taste in my mouth moving from bitter to acrid.

A nun had been killed. She'd been found strangled in the Claddagh church where she'd been saying her morning devotion. The papers put it down to some drug-crazed youth and lamented the state of the nation. I read the account with an icy chill in my gut. This was victim three.

When I finally got home, I was wired. I rang the Guards, got through to Clancy, shouted, 'Now will you pay attention?'

He waited a moment, then said, 'Ah, Taylor, conspiracies everywhere. We've already arrested a deranged person found with her rosary beads in his possession. Gold ones – he liked the shine on them. I think.'

I argued, 'It can't be him. There is a list – I showed you – already three from it are dead and the person who wrote that wasn't attracted by – ' I could barely contain myself, ' – something fucking shiny.'

He sniggered. 'Language, Taylor. What have you been drinking? The water? Tell you what – if your letter-writer puts your name on the list, we'll definitely pay attention. Might even buy him a few pints.'

I threw my mobile across the room.

I was beyond anger. I wanted to inflict serious damage on somebody. I was pacing up and down my small apartment, thinking, *Fuck 'em all. What do I care?*

Then the post arrived.

Lots of offers to join video clubs, one letter informing me I'd won a million euro and all I had to do was ring the following number, a voucher for a free pizza . . . and then a white envelope. I recognized the writing, tore it open, saw the one single page and the typed message that read:

> Three
> But who's counting?
> Benedictus

I pulled open my door and ran smack into my gay neighbour, who was trying to fit his key into his lock. He was hampered by a broken arm and a crutch, his face a riot of bruises and cuts.

I stammered, 'Jesus, what happened?'

He gave me a look of withering contempt. 'The gay-bashers. You said not to worry about them. But guess what? You were wrong.'

I felt dreadful. He had asked for help and what had I done but ignore him?

'Let me help you with that.' I pointed to the key.

He near spat, 'Help? I think I've had as much of your assistance as I'd ever want.'

'I'm so sorry.' I meant it.

He gave me his full attention. 'Indeed, you are – a sorry excuse for a human being.' Got his door open and slammed it in my face.

*　　　*　　　*

I went to The Quays on, yeah, Quay Street. I'd never had a drink there me whole life as it's regarded as a tourist haunt. I stepped up to the counter, ordered a large Jameson and a pint of stout. The barman – non-national, of course – poured the pint too fast and didn't let it settle, but I was in a hurry. Afraid I'd change my mind. I gave him a twenty, got fuck all back, and moved to a corner with a long wooden table – thought, *Good, I'll line it with empties.*

My hands had a slight tremble, but nothing too noticeable. I lifted the Jay, downed half, said, 'Welcome home.' Then I downed half the poor pint in one gulp and sat back. Let the magic begin, dark as it wished.

That first drink, you hear various responses. Most say the terrible guilt, the loss of sobriety, followed by the *if only* – if only they hadn't taken it. I felt like I'd finally let out my breath. For years, I'd been holding it and now . . . exhale . . . glorious. This was followed by false moments of exhilaration; I understood them for what they were and knew too that the reckoning would be ferocious, worse perhaps than before, but those first few minutes as the whiskey began to light a fire in my stomach felt worth it.

Ride the whirlwind, reap the wrath.

There is a certain peace – of the satanic variety, sure – but having given up the battle, it was done. No more aching, the struggle was over.

A guy approached, looked at me, went, 'Jack?'

It was Caz, a Romanian who'd been in Galway for nigh on a decade. He spoke English with an Irish lilt and knew more about the goings on in the city than any cop. Information was his ace and the more lurid, the better. We had a give-and-take relationship. I gave – usually twenty euro – and he took whatever he deemed the freight to be.

When the government deportations were at their most extreme, he always managed to evade the net, and now with the economy in threatened meltdown more non-nationals were due for the boot. But he was dressed in a flash leather jacket and crisp new jeans, and smelt of expensive cologne. Maybe he could give me twenty euro.

He said, 'Jesus, you're drinking.'

He'd managed to adopt the Irish habit of swearing without sounding as if he meant it – no mean achievement. I gave him my granite look, which translates as *So?*

Caz was way too wary to get into a confrontation with me. It was how he'd survived Galway for ten years. He shrugged. 'I just heard you'd been off it . . . a while.'

I finished the pint, said, 'And now I amn't off it.' I took out two twenties, handed them over, said, 'Get us a round.'

One twenty went into his pocket as he headed for the counter. He didn't need to ask for my order. I heard him call the barman a bollix and figured we'd get decent-drawn pints.

We did.

He didn't offer any change, raised his pint, touched mine, said, '*Sláinte.*'

'*Sláinte amach.*'

The added *amach* is reserved for close friends, implying warmth, and the Jay had given me the warmth.

Caz, foam lining his mouth, asked, 'Hear about the swamps?'

You have to be real old Galway to name them that. The swamps are a playing field close to Nimmo's pier.

I shook my head.

'Found arsenic in it and in three of the houses near by. The arsenic had been there for years, poisoning the poor bastards who lived there.'

86

I wasn't surprised. Horrified, sure, but surprised, no. They'd discovered asbestos in homes in Bohermore, and the number of birth abnormalities, not to mention a huge increase in Down syndrome, confirmed my belief that one way or another, the city officials were responsible. In the papers a professor of biology was saying that the virus currently in the water had been there for a decade!

I said, 'Speaking of poison, you know anything about gay-bashers?'

He looked to his left, fleetingly, enough to let me know he was going to lie, so I added, 'Don't fuck with me, mate. You know better, so let's not screw around.'

He smiled, drank some of his pint, then rubbed his thumb and forefinger together. I took out another twenty, held it on the table under my Jay, waited.

He took a furtive look round, then said, 'There's a guy named Gary Blake who has been shouting about ridding the town of heathens and perverts. He says first we take the homos, then we take Berlin, sorry, the child-molesters. GBH is his nickname. He plays golf with lots of the top guards.'

I ignored his lousy attempt at humour, the riff

on the Leonard Cohen song, echoed, 'GBH?'

He loved my ignorance. 'Grievous bodily harm. He uses homos for harm.'

'Where does he hang his hate shingle?'

Caz looked worried. 'Jesus, Jack, leave it alone, the guy is connected.'

I leaned across the table. 'Did I ask you if he was connected? You hear me ask that?'

He finished his drink, wanting to get away, not to be seen with me. Galway was a cosmopolitan city, but still in the valley of the squinting windows. He whispered, 'Newcastle Avenue, a new bungalow there.'

I sat back, the Jay stoking the old flames of rage and violence. It felt good, felt alive.

He added, 'Jack, he's one of the Blakes. They're, like, one of the tribes of Galway.'

I said, 'Time they were extinct, don't you think?'

He legged it fast.

I finished up. The temptation to stay was nigh on overwhelming, but I dragged me arse out of the comfortable position and thought, *Go home*.

I went back to my apartment and I dunno, maybe it was the booze but I thought I heard sobbing from behind my neighbour's door. That combined with the booze only made my resolve more determined. Inside my place, I pulled the small bookcase aside, took out an oilskin cloth, unwrapped it and took out the revolver.

When I'd had to cancel America, waiting on the result of Ridge's surgery, I'd found it hard to pass the time. A guy had asked me to help him clear out an old house, said, 'There'll be the price of a drink in it for you.'

Words to live by.

In the house, I'd found a torn copy of 'If' and what looked like an original Proclamation of Irish Independence, and in the oil rag, the old revolver. It was still functional, well cared for, five bullets with it. I imagined a Republican on the run, hiding out there. But what the fuck would he be doing with Kipling? I thought of the line in the poem:

> or being hated,
> don't give way to hating.

Is this what he said to himself at night? While he dreamed of harming his enemies?

Right.

It was why he had the revolver.

I'd put the two declarations on the bathroom wall and as I shaved in the morning would flick back and forth between the two ideologies. It made a sort of Irish sense, i.e. none.

I loaded the revolver with the five bullets, put it in my jacket, said, 'Let's rock 'n' roll.'

14

Funeral Path

Gary Blake's house was midway along Newcastle Avenue, the original name of the avenue being *Cosan an Aifreann*. Mass Path. Because the hearses from the morgue drove along this road to the funeral parlours. Newcastle Avenue didn't quite have the same ring to it.

The house had large wooden gates, but one was open and I went in. The small yard for parking was deserted and no lights were on. I rang the doorbell, and smiled at the nameplate on the door: St Jude's – the patron saint of hopeless cases.

I waited, then used my tool kit to open the door – a present from Stapelton, a psycho friend, long dead and by my hand.

I found myself in a long hall, with icons and pictures of avenging angels lining the walls and a huge blue banner that proclaimed: 'Aids is God's answer.'

I muttered, 'What's the question?'

The house was well cleaned and had one upstairs bedroom with a skylight. I opened the cupboard. Apart from a few shirts and jeans, it contained a baseball bat that looked well used – the smudges on the top weren't red paint – and a set of brass knuckles. Everything the urban vigilante required.

Downstairs again, I noticed a large bookcase with volumes on right-wing propaganda and numerous tomes on the scourge of homosexuality. I found a well-stocked drinks cabinet – I selected a bottle of Black Bushmills, got a heavy tumbler and poured myself a large one, had a sip and said, 'Now that is real fine.'

Glass in hand, I looked at the framed photos, all of the guy I presumed to be Blake. He had militia gear on in one, another showed him receiving a trophy for service to the community, and the final one showed him on a golf course with a number of men, one of whom I recognized as Superintendent Clancy. I went back to the kitchen and checked the fridge: full of choice meats, wines, lots of delicacies and a fresh salmon. I found a stick of French bread and made myself a thick sandwich. It went real well with the Bush.

I put my mini feast on the kitchen table, placed the revolver alongside and settled in to wait.

The food was so good, I was contemplating a second sandwich when the front door opened. There was a heavy footfall, then he walked into the kitchen, near jumping out of his skin when he saw me.

I asked, 'How was work, dear?'

He was in his late forties, slim build, pasty complexion with brown furtive eyes. Of course, you come home to find a guy at your kitchen table, eating your grub with a gun alongside, you're going to look furtive.

He took a moment, then blustered, 'Who the hell are you?'

I drained my glass, smiled in appreciation at the sheer quality of the booze and said, 'I'm serious fucking trouble.' I put my hand on the butt of the gun, said, 'Sit.'

He did.

I took the revolver in my left hand, swung the chamber out and let the five bullets tumble on to the table. I picked one up, put it in the chamber, smiled at Gary, then spun the chamber.

'I take it you've seen *The Deer Hunter*? Shit, macho guy like you, probably know it by heart.'

He had a light line of perspiration on his forehead as he asked, 'What is this all about?'

'Thing is, Gary – you don't mind if I call you Gary? – you've a real tidy home here, no sign of, how shall we say, *female occupancy*, and you're, lemme guess, in your late forties, not married, and in the fridge it's all fancy meats, nice wines, none of that Guinness or beer crap for you, so I'm wondering . . . are you gay? Got any Barbra Streisand albums, or is it Kylie now?'

His face contorted in rage. I waved the gun and he sat down as he spat, 'How dare you even utter that word in my house? They are a virus, a modern-day plague.'

I aimed the gun at him. 'And you're the cure?' I clicked the hammer back. 'I pull the trigger, you're gone.'

He nearly fell off the chair, stammered, 'You're deranged. God almighty, what is the matter with you?'

I said, 'It's real simple. I want you to retire

from the bashing gig.' I stood up, added, 'You now have to decide how serious I am.'

I leveled the revolver, said, 'They say I'm a drunk, and as you can see . . .' I indicated the dwindling Bushmills in the glass, '. . . I'm certainly partial to a wee dram. The thing is, how steady is my aim?'

I pulled the trigger and the bullet whizzed past his ear, leaving the tiniest nick on the rim, and lodged in the wall behind him. I was as shocked as he was, but had to appear nonchalant.

Jesus, an inch or so and I'd have blasted him right between the eyes. The tiny abrasion began to pump blood, which ran down the side of his neck.

I said, 'Next time, I'll be more accurate.'

He put his hand to his ear, checking to see if it was still attached, and muttered, 'Holy mother of God.'

I laughed. 'You'll need her if I hear of anything happening again.'

I went to the fridge, the gun held loosely in my hand, and took out the fresh salmon. I turned, gave him my best smile and said, 'Change your diet. Need to get some meat on you, pal.'

I took the fish with me.

I headed along the Newcastle Road, the fish under my arm, until I came to the Salmon Weir Bridge, where I threw the salmon into the water.

A young boy, maybe twelve, was watching me. 'Is that fish still alive?' he asked.

I lied, said, 'The water will revive him.'

He gave me a look of total contempt. 'The water is poisoned, it will kill him.'

He gave one more look into the water, hoping against hope, I think, then turned back to me.

'You're a very stupid man.'

Few would disagree.

15

Holy Water?

Next morning, I woke to my first hangover in years and go figure, it wasn't too bad. Sick stomach, sure, groggy head, par for the course. But nothing major. Not one of those biblical gigs where you swear, *Never again*.

I didn't think it was a whole new era. The real deal was coming down the pike but I was grateful for small mercies. I drank a half-litre of water, boiled the night before. It threatened to come right back up, then settled.

I shaved and only cut meself once. My eyes were red and there was a grey pallor on my face but it could have been worse.

I made some coffee and actually drank a cup. I didn't enjoy it much, but then I wasn't exactly looking for that. I wanted the caffeine hit. Where was it written that enjoyment would be part of the deal?

I dressed in a clean white shirt, cleanish jeans and a pair of Doc Martens I'd been breaking in for a while. Once you get past the new stage, few things are more comfortable.

I went out and knocked on my neighbour's door. He opened it cautiously. I said, 'I paid a visit to the guy who beat you up.'

He tried to read my face and then smiled. He had one of those radiant ones, like a child who still believes the world is good. 'Did you hurt him?'

'I stole his fish.'

He thought about that, then laughed. 'That's so *Godfather.* I love it.'

I shrugged and as I moved away he shouted, 'Party on, next Friday, bring anything but fish.'

He was a hard guy not to like.

I was up and out by noon the next day.

I started to walk along by O'Brien's Bridge, my heart light. I'd just reached the junction where you turn into Market Street when I almost collided with Father Malachy. He was the most dedicated smoker I know and was shrouded in a blizzard of smoke, as usual. He had enlisted my help when he had been threatened and his life was in danger and we had almost reached a state of friendly hostility. But it didn't last.

I stopped and looked at him.

'Taylor, by the holy, . . . do I smell drink on you? Ah, you're a hopeless case.'

I grabbed his arm. 'I helped you one time and you never paid me. You can pay me now by buying me a pint.'

He was going to protest, but Ireland had changed so much. A guy manhandling a priest wasn't going to bring the cavalry; in fact, it might well bring a lynch party.

I said, 'I need to talk to you.'

I indicated the short cut along by St Nicholas's Church and the pub across from it.

He said, 'I don't think you want to go in that place.'

I'd never been in. I knew it had changed hands many times, but then, hadn't everywhere? When I stared at him, he said, 'Your old friend works there.'

'Jeff?'

Jeff was the father of Serena May and the last

time we'd run into each other, he'd asked me if I was going after Cathy, his wife. Since then, I'd learnt that Cathy may have killed her own child. I wondered if he knew too. I said, 'That's not a problem,' and dragged him in.

A young barman was polishing glasses and two lone drinkers were sipping quietly at pints. No sign of Jeff.

I said to the young guy, 'Pint and a Jameson and whatever his holiness wants.'

He wanted tea and biscuits, if they had them.

The pub smelt fresh. Since the no-smoking ban had come in, this was one of the benefits.

Not for Malachy, though. He put his pack of Major – the strongest brand you can find – on the counter, with a box of Swan matches. He looked longingly at them, asked the barman, 'Do ye have a smoking room?'

The barman smiled. 'Yeah, sure, it's called the street.'

Not a devout Catholic then.

Malachy glared at him, muttered, 'Young pup.'

Finally the order came and we carried it over to a window table. We had a view of the church and I wondered if it bothered Malachy to be shadowed by a Protestant one.

He stirred the teapot, said, 'One lousy tea-bag. It must have broke their bloody hearts.'

I raised the pint and swallowed half. He gave me a look of pure disgust.

Before he could start, I said, 'I'm asking you again: what is benediction?'

He was dipping the biscuit in his weak tea and, distracted, lost half in the cup. 'What?'

'You heard me.'

He gazed in dismay at the soggy biscuit skimming the surface, then said, 'It's a blessing and also evening devotions, not that anyone goes any more. If you're looking for a blessing, you'd better ask someone else. You'll get none from me.'

I raised my glass of Jay. 'Glad to see you've mellowed in your old age. But why would, say, someone call themselves Benedictus?'

He pushed the whole ruined tea business aside and said, 'Because they're a lunatic.'

I had to agree he was probably right about that.

He stood up. 'I'm going for a fag.'

Any Americans within earshot would have been taken aback to hear that, though with all the clerical scandals, maybe not.

I said, 'You're forgetting something.'

He looked round and I added, 'Paying. Even priests have to pay now. You had it free long enough.'

He moved to the counter, gave the bar guy a bollocking about the tea and then came back. 'No wonder there's no one here, the prices they charge.'

I drained my drink and followed him outside.

He lit up, coughed and I asked, 'Give me one.'

He considered, then said, 'Buy your own.' And stomped off in a haze of self-satisfied smoke, like a fuming devil.

16

Restless Wind

I'd been listening to Billy Joe Shaver. His legendary album *Restless Wind* was on the track called 'Fit To Kill And Going Out In Style' when my mobile rang. It was Stewart. He sounded almost excited, if a Zen devotee could ever rise to that.

He said, 'I've some news.'

'Yeah?'

'We need to meet. I'm in the Meyrick, I'll buy you a coffee.'

Coffee. Like fuck.

I asked, 'Where the hell is the Merrick?' Not even knowing I was spelling it wrong.

He laughed. 'I keep forgetting that old

Galway gig of yours. It used to be the Great Southern Hotel.'

'Then why the hell didn't you say so? See you there in ten minutes.'

A few days had gone by since my visit to Gary Blake and there had been no reports of gay-bashing.

I'd found a temporary way to avoid complete alcoholic meltdown: an eye-opener at noon, then four pints and shorts in the evening. Ten drinks a day. It was holding, barely. I was never completely out of the game, but never quite with it, either. The time was coming when I'd lose count, literally, and just not give a fuck. Then watch out. I'd even gone to Jeff's pub a few times, looking for what – confrontation, affirmation, forgiveness? But no Jeff so far.

I put on my all-weather Garda coat, item 8234. They still wanted it back. Dream on. I wore a black sweatshirt for that rugged look and black jeans; the Doc Martens, of course.

Did I look dangerous? Yeah, if an old guy with a hearing aid and a limp scares you. I had great teeth, mind you. Not my own, but at least they shone. Something needed to.

The Meyrick looked the same as the old

Southern. Stewart was sitting in a plush leather armchair, glancing at *The Irish Times*. The headlines screamed about a coming election and the Taoiseach's money problems. The previous September he had come clean in a moving TV interview about, yes, getting a digout from friends when he was hurting financially, and the confession, instead of bringing him down, had led to a soar in popularity and the term *digout* had become local lore. These fresh allegations were proving harder to shake.

Stewart put the paper aside, hailed a passing waiter, ordered herbal tea for himself and looked to me.

I said, 'Pint and a Jameson, no ice.'

Stewart raised an eyebrow and I warned, 'Don't start.'

He didn't.

I sat down and looked at him. He was the picture of tranquillity – expensive suit, knotted silk tie, shoes of the softest leather I'd ever seen. I asked, derision in my voice, 'Tell me again what it is you actually do, now that you're out of the drug business?'

A slight frown creased his eyes, then he let his face relax. The dope reference reminded him naturally of his six years' jail time, but I guess the Zen kicked in and he smiled. 'I trade information, nothing more valuable. It's not what you know but knowing what it is that is where the information lies.'

Jesus.

The drinks came and Stewart said, 'Put it on my account.'

His account.

I refrained from rising to the bait, took a hefty wallop of the Jay, sat back and waited for it to jolt. It always did, so far. I asked, 'What's the news, or do I have to pay for the information?'

He was bulletproof now, knew my moves too well. He made a grand show of fussing with the tea, then poured. It smelt like dandelions. Maybe it was.

He said, 'I've spent two weeks researching our Benedictus.'

Our?

He continued, 'You have to look behind the actions to discover the motivation, and there is always, no matter how obscure or twisted, a reason. Now we have a guard, a judge and a nun. Two elements stand out – revenge or punishment, or indeed both – so you dig a little deeper to see how these three people are connected, random though they appear, and lo and behold, a person begins to emerge, very slowly, out of the shadows. You go back into court records, newspapers, and the puzzle starts to take shape.' He stopped.

I drank some of the Guinness – it tasted real fine on the back of the Jay – and asked, 'So who is he?'

That irritating smile again. 'Wrong question.'

Maybe if I leaned over, gave him a slap in the mouth, he'd tell me the right one.

I said, 'I give up. Tell me.'

'Not he. She.'

Took me a moment to grasp. 'You're sure?'

He sipped at the wretched tea – no one is ever going to convince me they like that crap.

Then he said, 'Here's a scenario: a young girl is viciously raped, goes before the courts, and two guards testify. The judge throws out the case, due to lack of evidence. The girl throws herself in the Corrib a week later. Now here is the interesting part. Her sister, a nun, leaves the convent. There is a suggestion she was asked to go due to the scandal involving her sister, and the nun's name in Holy Orders . . . yeah, you guessed it, Sister Benedictus.'

I muttered, 'Jesus.'

Stewart looked quietly pleased with himself. 'Her real name is Josephine Lally, known as Jo. The smart one in the whole sordid case was the rapist. He took off for parts unknown and can't be found, so I guess that's why he's not on the list.'

It made total sense.

He watched me, then said, 'And before you ask, I spoke to the Mother Superior – she didn't outright admit that the nun was fired or whatever they do with nuns – I suppose defrock would hardly be right. I asked her where Jo was now and gee, no idea.'

I had to know. 'How did you get to see the Mother Superior?'

He smiled. 'I posed as a priest, and I had the air of quietness and humility that nuns think priests should have. I was very convincing, and all you need to know is, nuns love priests.'

I could see him in the role; he had all the moves and with the Zen gig, he was a natural. I was impressed. I didn't say so, he was impressed enough with himself. I said, 'So all we have to do is find her.'

He was shaking his head.

I snapped, 'What?'

'We have to prove it.'

It was my turn to smile, the booze giving me a swagger I hadn't felt in a long time. 'We find her, I'll prove it.'

He stood up, said, 'Jack, the way you're drinking, I'd be surprised if you could find your way out of the hotel.'

And he was gone.

17

Pint of Ferocity

I met up with Ridge that evening. She was surprised when I suggested Garavan's, one of the unchanged pubs in the heart of the city, and she went, 'Jack, I'm not drinking.'

I said, 'Who was talking about you?' And hung up.

Walking down Shop Street, a busker was playing 'Carrickfergus'. I was only a few yards from the pub but I stopped and listened to my heritage, my past, calling and cajoling through the ferocious sadness of that song. I put ten euro in the guy's cap and he winked, said, 'God and His family bless you.'

I was early for Ridge, to get a few in before she could lecture me. I was working on me third pint when she arrived. She looked well: white jeans, black T-shirt and black short jacket; her hair was shining and her eyes were clear as water. Well, not Galway water. I'd grabbed one of the snugs, little alcoves where you have privacy.

She stared at my pint for a full minute, then asked, 'When did this nonsense begin again?'

The earlier pints had me in gear and I said, 'A week ago you were sucking out of a bottle first thing in the morning. You couldn't tell your arse from your elbow, so don't lecture me, girl.'

She sat and I toned it down a bit. 'Get you anything?' I asked.

Got the glare, which I took as a no.

'So, report,' I said.

She seemed like she might actually strike me and she was well capable. 'Report . . . are you codding me? I don't report to you. I did you a favour, that's all. I don't work for you.'

I raised my glass. 'Cheers, then.'

Was I deliberately antagonizing her? You betcha.

We sat in grim silence till she said, 'I went out there. Lovely people and the young girl was a delight. She told me one of the stable hands had been fired a month ago, so I checked him out – and guess what? He recently bought a supply of hay and horse feed.'

I was delighted. Jesus, two cases cracked in one day – this called for celebration. I stood up. 'Terrific, let me get you something, you did great.'

She didn't answer so I went to the bar and got a large Jay. A guy at the counter said, 'That's a nice young wan you got there.'

I paid for the drink, said, 'Trust me, nice she isn't.'

As I got back to Ridge, she was preparing to leave. I asked, 'So when do we go get this stable hand?'

She gave me a look of contempt. 'I called the Guards. They arrested him an hour ago and recovered the pony.'

I nearly dropped the drink. 'You let the fecking Guards take the credit?'

Now she smiled, with no trace of warmth or humour. 'That's their job, and it doesn't hurt my chances of returning to the force.'

I was raging. 'We could have spun it out, made a nice few bob from that Anglo-Irish guy – he's loaded.'

She glanced at my double Jay and said, 'And so are you.'

18

Friendship of the Damned

I lost two weeks.

My last conscious memory is being in the pub where Jeff worked, and finally we got to meet. I was well en route to oblivion, skipping the Guinness, just nose into the Jameson when he appeared. He was dressed much as he always had been: the black 501s, granddad shirt and the waistcoat – what the Americans call a vest – and the long grey hair tied in a ponytail. Our previous encounters, I'd been totally contrite, taken whatever lashing he had to give and he'd had plenty.

Not any more.

Not only did I have the back-up of most of a litre of booze in my gut, but I also had the knowledge that I wasn't responsible for the death of his child. Lethal combination.

He said, 'Jack, I heard you'd been in.'

Jesus, was that an almost friendly tone? For one brief moment, I remembered the warm, close friendship we'd had. But the madness that was building overrode the memory and I said, 'I was beginning to think you were a rumour paraded as a fact.'

He smiled. 'Always the way with a turn of phrase.'

I asked, 'How's the missus?'

Like a punch in the face and I knew he knew. Pain leaked from his eyes, cancelling the brief smile. He asked, 'Got a minute to talk? Over in the corner there, bit of quiet.'

I said, 'Always got time for an old friend, right? Why don't you do some bar stuff, like get me a jar, and I'll get us some seats. How would that be, old buddy?'

I cringe now at the recollection and I'd love to plead I didn't mean it.

Sure I did.

He nodded and headed behind the bar. I grabbed some seats, feeling the very worst thing a person can feel and certainly the most danger-ous – feeling self-righteous.

I'd say *God forgive me* but it seems pointless when I can't forgive myself.

Jeff returned with a Jameson and a mug of coffee, a logo on the side proclaiming, *Is bheannacht an obair* (blessed is the work).

Whatever you might say about God, he sure likes a good laugh.

I wondered if the murderous ex-nun out there would appreciate the irony. Jeff sat and put the drink before me, refraining from commenting about my drinking. He said, 'So, you've heard the story about Cathy and—' he had to gulp, as if his air was cut off before he could say the name of his child, 'Serena May.'

I knew it wasn't his fault, what had happened, but no way, no fucking way was I cutting him any slack. The years of guilt and grief I'd endured and he was there, in front of me.

I asked venomously, 'And when were you planning on letting me know that I wasn't responsible? All the fucking times you threatened me – remember those, buddy?' I had to pause to catch my breath, I was so enraged. 'When exactly were you going to say, "Gee, sorry, pal, I was wrong"? Or were you hoping I wouldn't hear? That we could just forget about it and, what's the buzz word? Fucking *move on*? Just one of those things that happens, but what the hell, time healeth all and let's, what, count the fucking days to Christmas?'

He hung his head and muttered, 'Jack, when I heard, it nearly killed me. I still can't grasp it. I—'

I stood up and asked, 'Where's the murderous bitch now?'

His head came up, the eyes momentarily flashed, and I thought, *You poor bastard, you still love her.*

Then he said, 'She's in treatment. They say it will take a long time.'

I picked up the glass, the amber liquid catching the light from the street, like a moment's sad grace. I said, 'Thank God, she's being taken care of. You tell her I wish her a speedy fucking recovery and I look forward to seeing her. And this . . .' I indicated the glass, poured the whiskey slowly on the floor, letting each drop lash his heart, 'This you can shove up yer arse.'

19

Retribution

I came to – or rather, was kicked to – by the side of the canal. I opened my eyes to see three teenagers in hoods standing over me, one going, 'Get up, yah old wino.'

Jesus, I was sick. If they ever have an Olympic event for hangovers, I'm gold. This was a beauty.

The second hoodie was lighting matches, flicking them at me. I touched my ear – the hearing aid was gone, but I could hear this little bastard. The third leant over, said, 'Fucker smells like piss.'

They were having a high old time. When they decided to throw me in the water, it would have been a relief. But I reached out, grabbed one of them by his foot, got up on one knee, and in pure sickness and rage, lifted him up and threw him in the canal.

The other two stared in stunned silence.

I croaked, 'Who's next?'

Before they could take off, I grabbed the second, spasms of nausea doubling me, and managed to shake the bollocks. Out of his pockets fell my wallet, keys and hearing aid.

The other one was pleading, 'We was only messing, mister.'

The one in the water was clinging on to a piece of driftwood. I kicked the remaining kid in the balls, went through his pockets, had to stop mid search, vomited all over him, got his wallet and finally straightened up. My body was in total agony but the rush of violence had energized me. I leaned over the first one and growled, 'Where's my watch?

On his wrist.

I broke two of his fingers out of pure vindictiveness.

My limp was acting up, and as I began to hobble away, I saw an old-age pensioner leaning against a wall, smoking a pipe, the picture of contentment. He said, 'I've waited a long time to see something as mighty as that.'

I looked back. The one in the water was struggling now and I asked the old guy, 'You think he's drowning?'

He took a long pleasurable pull at the pipe and said, 'Please God.'

I made my shaky way along the end of the canal and turned on to what passes in that area for the main street. I stopped at an off-licence, ignored the guy holding his nose and got a half pint of Jay. I said, 'Looks like rain, you think?'

He didn't think anything, least not with me.

I had to stop halfway up the street as another spasm gripped my stomach. I gritted my teeth and got home. Once inside, I collapsed, sweat coursing down me and the smell of my own body turning my stomach even more. Lying doubled up on the floor, I managed to pry the top off the bottle and gulp some whiskey down.

I waited for it to kick in and when it did, was able to open my eyes. There on the table was my mobile phone. I could see the message light blinking even though the battery had worn down. I did a hasty check: nineteen messages.

I crawled to the shower, tore off my reeking clothes and scalded myself for ten minutes, then took another belt of the Jay. Needed to before I checked the mirror.

Christ, it was bad: a shaggy beard, cuts and bruises all down my cheeks, a black eye that had turned yellowish blue.

I put the clothes in the bin, went to my underwear drawer and, God be praised, found three sleeping pills. I took them all with one more gulp of the whiskey and climbed, shivering, into bed. With any luck, I'd never wake up.

This hangover I was going to sleep through, come hell or high water or both. This hangover was going to be biblical.

It lasted ten days, but who's counting?

Days of nightmare, sweats and horror. I'd not so much wake as come to, drenched in perspiration, seeing rats gnawing at my feet, screaming, 'They're not there.' Didn't stop me from trying to beat them off with the handle of a brush, all the while whimpering and crying like a lost angel. Serena May came too, heading the line of the dead, all accusing, all reaching out with wasted limbs, reaching to bring me with them, and me howling, 'I'm already there.'

And behind the procession of the departed,

always, a shadowy nun, singing like a nursery rhyme, *Catch me if you can.*

There were odd moments, days, I don't know, of partial lucidity, when I'd stagger out, needing a tiny drop of whiskey just to get dressed and buy food, knowing I had to have something in my system. Most of it came back up. Still, I persisted.

The day I got by on one mouthful of booze, I knew the worst was over. Physically, anyway. The guilt, the mental torture, I was too fucked to be able to recoil under its lash. It could wait; it usually did.

Noon, how many days later I had no idea, I opened my eyes, sheets twisted round my neck like a shroud, and felt better. I moved off the bed, which reeked to high heaven of – well, you can imagine. My legs were shaky and for a moment I thought, *I'm not able to walk*, but then they began to steady and I got to the bathroom. And there I was. A full grey beard had grown. My eyes, though shadowed, were clearing, the awful sickness had left them. I got into the shower and for over half an hour I scrubbed like a demented thing. Finally, I emerged, scaled to the core but clean. I shaved off the beard and my hand had only had the vaguest tremble. The lone whiskey bottle had maybe two inches left but I ignored it.

I made some tea, scrambled some eggs, added burnt toast and got most of it down. I gathered up my ruined clothes, put them in the washer and found, as Kristofferson sang, my cleanest dirty shirt, and a pair of jeans I'd never worn as they'd been too tight. Now they hung off me like an abandoned prayer. I had to tie my belt twice round to hold them up.

I charged the phone and found one of Stewart's pills, which I took, not knowing what the hell it was. Twenty minutes later, I was mellowing out.

When the phone was ready, I took a deep breath and clicked on the messages. Six from Ridge – where the hell was I? – and eight from Stewart, insisting I call him. His last call said, 'I've found her.'

The ex-nun?

Then a voice I didn't recognize came on. There must have been a handkerchief over the mouthpiece to disguise the voice, but it was definitely a woman.

'Ah Jack, you have been a biblical disappointment. You sank into the pit and so are no longer a worthy adversary. May the Lord leave you in the inferno of your own making. Your friend, ah, he was so clever and I very nearly underestimated him, but his own ingenuity led by pride caused, shall we say, his loss of focus. I got your number from him, albeit unwillingly. God spoke, as I prepared to send him to his Maker I heard the Word, and so he was spared. God's ways are not ours, he should have died, And he will, if he continues to meddle. *Salve et genuflectis.* I have his phone, I have your number, *sea secundis mea.* Benedictus.'

Jesus, chilled me to the bone.

I rang Stewart's number. No dial tone, nothing.

I grabbed my coat, got moving.

Stewart lived in a small terraced house near Cooke's corner. I rang the doorbell for five minutes. Finally a man looked out of the house next door and said, 'That young lad just went to the shops.'

I waited and finally here he was, dressed in a fine suit as usual, but with a fading bruise on his forehead.

He smiled, said, 'Ah, Maigret shows up, if a little late.'

I didn't know what to say.

'How are you?'

Seemed so inadequate.

He said, his voice strangled, 'I found our nun, but in retrospect, I think she found me.'

He took out his keys and we went in. His house reeked of patchouli.

He said, 'I'm going to make some tea, and if you really need a drink, there's a bottle of gin in the cupboard.'

Jesus, I needed it, but I said, 'Some bottled water might be good.'

He brought that, had a mug of some herbal stuff for himself and without preamble launched in. 'She has a brother, and on a hunch – isn't that what you *detectives* call them? – I went to his home, rang the bell and heard a woman say, "Come on in, the door is open." It was. The same voice said, "I'm upstairs." I was halfway up when out of nowhere she hit me with something – a hurley, do nuns play hurling? Maybe a hockey stick. Hurt though.'

I had no comment so he continued in almost a bantering tone, 'I did what you do, I fell down the stairs. I couldn't see, but I could sense her standing over me, and then she sprinkled what she said was holy water over me, to cleanse me.

Oh, she had a knife – lethal-looking thing – and looked like she was about to – how should I put it? – finish the job, when her head turned, as if she was listening to someone. Then she said, "Your time has not yet come." And she blessed me in Latin – that really helped. I tell you, Jack, whoever spoke to her, God freaking bless 'em.'

He let me digest that and then added, 'I had me one serious headache for a few days. Oh . . . and she stole my phone. Isn't that, like, against nuns' rules?'

'I'm so sorry.'

He gave what could have been a laugh and said, 'Odd, she said the same thing – that she was sorry.'

'What can I do?'

He seemed to be checking the various permutations of that, then said, 'Go find her.'

I stood up, tried again. 'It's my fault, Stewart.'

I was at the door before he said, 'Isn't it always?'

20

Sisters in Arms

I finally kicked into gear. It was like I was so caught up in so many mind storms, any instincts I ever had were closed down. But now a thought hit me. I rang Stewart and he answered with, 'Already?

He sounded testy, the Zen not up to its usual standard or more than likely, me.

I said, 'Sorry to be a nuisance, but when you went to see the Mother Superior, did she mention our psycho friend being close to any other nun in the convent?'

'I did take some notes after. Give me a moment.'

I tried to curb my impatience and then he was back. 'Good thinking, Jack. She was tight with a Sister Maeve, though I don't know, can you say nuns are *tight*?'

Tight is frequently used in Ireland to describe someone who's either mean or drunk, sometimes both. Few things worse, I suppose, than a tight drunk.

I said, 'Depends whether they were drinking buddies.'

He ignored that, said, 'Sister Maeve teaches in the Mercy Primary School and that's located—'

I cut him off, snapped, 'I know where the fucking school is.'

There was an intake of breath and then he said, 'Real pleasure to help you, Jack, you're so grateful.'

And he rung off.

21

Lord Have Mercy

I headed for the Mercy.

And I know, *mercy* seemed to be a scarce commodity, like clean water.

Nuns as teachers were becoming a rarity – most of the schools used lay people now. I headed for the admin office and a very friendly young lady behind a desk gave me a nice smile and asked, 'Might I help you?'

Niceness confuses me. I'm so accustomed to barbed banter that genuine warmth throws me. I gave her my best smile back, hoped it didn't look too much like a grimace, and asked, 'Would it be possible to see Sister Maeve?'

She picked up the phone. 'Might I ask what it's in connection with?'

'We're having a fundraiser and her name came up as someone who might suggest the most deserving charitable causes.'

Another lovely smile. 'Oh, she's the best fund-raiser. Everyone consults with Sister Maeve.'

My turn to try another smile. It was making my jaw ache. I said, 'I've come to the right place, then.'

She spoke on the phone, then put it down and said, 'Your lucky day – she's free for the next hour. Home Ec was cancelled.'

'Home Ec?'

She laughed as if I was just a fun guy. 'Home Economics. The girls learn to cook and run a home.'

I was going to add that the fast-food joints littering the town might be the reason for the absence of skills, but didn't want to push my luck.

The girl said, 'She'll be down in a moment. She's just fixing her make-up.'

Was she kidding?

Nuns . . . make-up?

She added, 'You'll love Sister Maeve. Every-body does.'

I tried to contain my excitement.

The girl was in the mood to chat and

asked, 'When is the fundraiser?'

I was saved from yet another lie by the appearance of the nun.

I don't know what I was expecting – at the very least a habit, cowl, etc. Nope. She was dressed in a smart jumper and skirt and low-heeled patent shoes, and looked all of twenty. What is it with nuns? They never seem to age. Not a line on her face. She had one of those open Irish faces – no guile or subterfuge had inhabited it. She was almost pretty, if lively eyes and a mischievous smile count.

She extended her hand and I saw the wedding band. I'd forgotten they're married to God. She said, 'I'm Maeve.'

A little bewildered, I asked, 'I don't call you Sister?'

Her eyes twinkled and she said, 'Not unless it's absolutely necessary.'

I said, 'I'm Jack Taylor.'

Her grip was warm and strong as she asked, 'You drink coffee, Mr Taylor?'

Jesus, I nearly quipped, *Does a bear shit in the woods?* Said, 'Yes, and please, it's Jack.'

She turned to the girl, said, 'I'll back in an hour. If anyone asks, I'm gone on a date.'

The girl loved that.

Outside, I thought for one awful moment she was going to link arms, but she just said, 'Let's go to Java, they have the best cappuccino – lots of chocolate sprinkle, and they give you a free biscuit too.'

'Works for me.'

We got a table by the window and she said, 'Oh, this is such a treat for me.'

Christ, I felt bad. She was truly a nice person and here I was, about to ask her literally murderous questions.

We ordered coffee and what the hell, I had the cappuccino, chocolate sprinkle and all.

When it came she said, 'I never know whether to go for the biscuit first or have the coffee.'

Well, before the shit hit the fan I could at least be civil. I said, 'You ever try dunking?'

She hadn't, but did, tasted it and exclaimed, 'Oh that's perfect. You do know your sweeties, Mr Taylor – I mean Jack.'

I was sure glad no one who knew me could hear that last comment.

She took another sip of coffee, relished it, then folded her fingers and said, 'I'm all yours, Jack.'

Was she flirting with me?

Time to 'fess up.

I said, 'I lied to you.'

'About the dunking?'

I wish.

I was as close to squirming as I've ever come. I plunged on. 'This is not about charity. I'm here about Josephine Lally – Sister Benedictus?'

Her eyes lost their twinkle and causing that to occur jolted my heart. She gave me a long look, then asked, 'Are you a policeman?'

Then before I could answer, she suddenly had a thought and her eyes lit up. Not, alas, with joy, but remembrance. She said, 'Jack Taylor . . . Oh my Lord, Jo talked about you.'

I was about to speak, but she help up her hand, the gold band on her finger catching a stray ray of sun through the window, almost like a shard of hope. I was interrupting her train of thought. Then she said, 'Yes, her sister. Oh, poor tragic Siobhan . . .'

She made the sign of the cross, then said, 'Siobhan was raped, I believe in the most brutal way possible.' She shuddered. 'There was of course a trial and the two guards were maybe more involved than was said. I don't like to cast aspersions but they definitely played a part and the rapist was exonerated, charges dismissed.'

She had to stop to compose herself. I could see the toll it was taking on her and I realized that the two guards who had been killed were the two bastards involved. What the fuck had the judge been thinking?

As if she read my thoughts, she said, 'The judge, may God forgive him, commended the guards on their diligence and devotion to justice.'

Jesus Christ, no wonder the two guards were on the killer's list – and the damn judge, he sure belonged on it. I'd have gone after all three myself.

'Then Siobhan . . . as you know, took her own life. That put Jo right over the precipice and she started to babble in voices, telling me that God would extract justice in this world and that He had selected His instrument. Mother Superior tried to get her to seek professional help and she blew up. There was a terrible scene and she was asked to leave the convent.'

She was weeping now. I was afraid to offer her a tissue lest she stop the flow of the story – I had to hear it. She was nearly done.

'The last time I saw her, she was packing her meagre belongings and had a sheet of paper in her hand. She said, in the most chilling voice I've ever heard, "I shall be the instrument of the Lord." I tried to give her a hug – she was my sister in all the ways that really matter – but she flinched when I touched her and said, "Benedictus will not be touched, but will, by the mighty wrath of God, touch all those who caused the death of the innocent." I never saw her again.'

Her coffee had gone cold, and the remains of the biscuit floated near the surface like defeated dreams.

'But why is she targeting me?' I asked her. The drive for revenge on all who had wronged her sister was clear enough. But me? What was my part in all of this?

Sister Maeve stood up abruptly. 'I must get back to my class.'

And she was gone.

Part Two

'If you work on your mind with your mind, how can you avoid an immense confusion?'

Seng-Ts'an

Part Two

22

Loaded

Next morning I'm energized, gulp down some coffee, literally gallop out of my flat.

Stewart gave me the address of Benedictus's brother, so I head for his house. Maybe he knows where she is now. And if he doesn't tell me, I'll beat the fucking daylights out of him and enjoy it.

I knock on the door. I have the revolver in me right pocket. If she comes at me with a hockey stick, I'll blow the cunt to smithereens. Sorry for the language, but I'm spitting iron over the hurt to Stewart.

I hear real heavy footsteps. The door opens on the most overweight man I've ever laid eyes on. I mean, 300 lbs and change. He's wearing what appears to be a blue tent and it's lined with sweat.

He puffs, 'May I help you?'

The butt of the revolver is sweaty in my hand and I let go lest I shoot me balls off from nerves.

'I'm looking for your sister.' Let lots of aggression into my tone.

He sighs, more like a rumble, says, 'Taylor . . . Jack Taylor. It is, isn't it?'

I nod and he waves me in. He doesn't walk so much as waddle and we go into a surprisingly neat front room, and he flops down in the largest chair I've seen.

He says, 'I had to have it made special and it cost. Would you like a drink? You'll have to get it yourself – in the cabinet there, and some water for me. I'm trying to cut back.'

He laughs at the sheer ridiculousness of this. He has a warm, embracing laugh. I'm trying not to like him.

Fuck it. I pour me a large Bushmills. When do you come across fifty-year-old black Bushmills? I get him a bottle of Galway water and a glass – all the glasses are clean and shining. I hand the glass to him and I sit in a hard chair opposite him.

He raises his glass, toasts, 'Chin chin . . . and I've enough chins for both of us.'

I knock back the golden dram – heaven in a liquid – and he adds, 'My name is Benedict.' Let that hover, then says, 'Yes, she stole the name. She is indeed Benedictus and quite truly insane. She didn't always use to be.'

He gulps the water – some dribbles down his multi-chins. He continues, 'But then a lot of us used to be sane. Wouldn't you agree?'

I still can't get over his almost childlike voice, so soft, so quiet.

I say, 'I need to find her.'

He nods, says, 'You'd better.'

Hello? I ask, 'What does that mean?'

'It means she is obsessed with you.'

'Why?'

He shakes his head. 'She never told me, and trust me, Mr Taylor, she is not somebody you can interrogate.'

My hand is back on the revolver. I'm losing my bearings. I take a swig of the gold liquid, croak, 'What?'

'After Siobhan's suicide and Jo got slung out of the order, she went completely wild. Got tattoos – can you believe it? – and very elaborate ones. But in her latest stage of insanity, she

143

skinned them off. And I mean that literally. She's into pain, as you're about to discover.'

It took me a while to digest this and all the while he watched me, sweat pouring down his face. He didn't attempt to wipe it off. He had the softest brown eyes, like a cocker spaniel.

I finally managed to ask, 'Why didn't you do something about it – about her – when you realized she was actually out there, killing people?'

He looked me right in the eyes, no guile or evasion. 'Because I'm afraid of her.' He paused, then said, 'You'd better be afraid of her too. She has, as the Yanks term it, a *hard on* for you . . . if that's not too disrespectful to say about a nun.'

And then he began to pull himself out of the chair. I rose to help but he waved me away. He got some more water and the bottle of Bush, handed it to me, said, 'Please, have another.'

I did.

He sank back into the chair with visible relief.

I had to know, asked, 'Why me?'

He finished the water and said, 'You killed a child, and worse, a handicapped child.'

I was going to protest, tell him of the new

developments. Instead I said, 'We'll have to stop her.'

He gave a small titter – that's the only way I can describe the sound. 'We? Not me, mate. As you can see, getting out of a chair is the biggest accomplishment of my day, and going after Jo – whoa, not me, fellah.'

'But you're her brother. Don't you feel any responsibility?'

He suddenly grabbed his shoulder and began to intone, '*It is related in the annals of Clairvaux that St Bernard asked Our Lord which was His greatest unrecorded suffering and Our Lord answered, "I had on my shoulder, while I bore my Cross on the Way of Sorrows, a grievous wound which was more painful than the others and which is not recorded by men."*'

I was thinking, *What the fuck?* and more. Whacko.

Sweat was now flooding his body and he tore at the fabric on his shoulder, gasped, 'Come, Mr Taylor, come and see the work of Sister Benedictus.'

Like a damn fool, I did.

I've seen wounds, cuts, abrasions, from knives, guns, hatchets, hurleys, and none of them pretty. But this . . . this was a whole other territory. A huge gash had been gouged into his shoulder, as if with a machete, and then looked as if it had been hammered with a blunt instrument. It had that look of something that had healed and been re-opened.

It made me sick to my stomach. Not even Bushmills, potent as it is, could block the sheer horror of it. And I swear, it smelt of corruption. I stammered, 'You need to get that looked at.'

I didn't want to mention gangrene, but I'd seen green in there.

He gave the saddest smile I've seen, said, ''Tis my penance.'

Like I said, whacko.

So I asked, 'What happened?'

He looked at his water glass. Empty. And his eyes read, *How'd that happen?*

I went and got him another – fuck it, two of them. Poured me some water too. My throat was parched. Handed them to him and he said, 'You are a kind man, Mr Taylor. Behind that tough-guy mask there is a good person lurking, but it won't save you from my sister. As you can see, it hasn't saved me.'

'How will I find her?'

He gulped more water. 'You won't have to. She's already tracking you.'

'Have you a photo?'

He gave a loud belly laugh. 'Nuns don't do snaps.'

I nearly snapped meself, but held it back. 'You must have some idea where she'd hole up? And for Chrissake, what is she doing for money?'

He said calmly, 'The Lord provides.'

Jesus, the temptation to wallop him was ferocious.

He said, 'You wish to strike me, Mr Taylor?'

Fuck.

He let his eyes close for a moment. The sweat must have been stinging the bejaysus out of them. 'Don't feel bad, Mr Taylor. People have wanted to strike me my whole life. They see me, my massive bulk, and it brings out something very ugly in them.'

I couldn't resist, said, 'Weight Watchers – you ever heard of them dudes? Instead of wallowing in self-pity, you could do something about yourself.'

I know . . . from me, priceless.

He opened his eyes, a shine in them now, said, 'And you could go to AA.'

Touché.

He added, 'You think it's food that has me like this? It's a medical condition. Sure, I can go on diets and I've tried them all. I even drank cabbage soup for a month, nothing else, and in fact I put on weight. Children call me names on the streets – you know how that feels. In this new rich country of ours obesity is becoming a national issue, so at least I won't be alone.'

This was going nowhere. I stood up and asked, 'You're not going to help, then? You're just going to let her run amok?'

He gave that smile again. 'But I have you on the case, Mr Taylor. What more could the city need?'

23

Child of Fate

She felt strange wearing the nun's habit again but there was no better disguise. She had come to the most vital part of the list.

The crux, as it were.

The child.

It was laughable how easy it was to snatch him.

She had gone to the house and there, playing in the garden, was the little boy. She could see a woman inside, chatting on the phone. She'd taken the little boy by the hand. Even at that young age, he knew nuns were to be trusted.

She had a bar of Cadbury's Dairy Milk, the large one, which she'd laced with the contents of her sleeping pills. By the time she got him back to her refuge, he was already falling asleep.

She wrapped him in a blanket and laid him on the marble floor, a heater beside him. She didn't want him to catch cold.

Least not before she cut his throat.

24

Answers

A guard was killed in a 'freak accident'. The brakes on his car failed and he hit a tree. He died on impact.

I crossed him off her list.

We were getting down to the wire.

In desperation, I decided to return to Sister Maeve. There had to be more I could learn. I dreaded going back; she had told me in no uncertain terms that she didn't wish to see me again, but I'd been told that by most everyone I knew.

I entered the Mercy School and I swear, my heart was pounding. The girl who'd been at reception the last time had been so warm and friendly. I expected her to call the guards this time.

She didn't.

'Mr Taylor, terrific. Sister Maeve has been trying to find a way to contact you.'

What do you know?

She picked up the phone, had a brief conversation, then put it down and said, 'Sister will see you now. Her office is on the first floor.'

Office?

I climbed the flight and my limp objected, but not too much. The door to her office was open and she rose from behind a cluttered desk to greet me. 'Mr Taylor, please close the door.'

I did.

She indicated the hard chair opposite her desk and she looked seriously worried. I felt like an errant student facing the principal. She no longer had the twinkle in her eye and she actually wrung her hands. 'I don't know how to begin.' She sighed then said, 'I've met with Jo.'

I was going to shout, 'Did you call the Guards?' But I went with, 'When?'

She was now in deep distress. 'A few days ago, she told me she had a confession to make and as she no longer trusted the Church, she had chosen me to hear it. Not for absolution, she said, but to set the record straight.'

She paused to let me digest this, see if I had any comment.

I didn't.

She continued, 'Jo told me that she had been with a man before she joined the convent. In fact, because of that, she joined. She had . . . *lain* with him and then found herself pregnant. Back then, it was difficult to be an unmarried mother. She went to England.'

That could mean only one thing: abortion. No wonder the poor woman was unhinged.

'Did she try approaching the man?'

Her hands were now twisted round each other. She wouldn't look at me.

Took me a moment and then it all came together. I blurted, '*Me?* Ah, for Jesus's sake, you think I wouldn't remember that?'

Maeve gave me the first direct look since I'd sat down. 'She said you were an alcoholic even then and suffered blackouts. You had no memory of the event.'

Oh God Almighty, this was true. Harsh, bitter truth. From almost the beginning of my drinking, I had always been subject to blackouts. Then an even more horrendous realization struck me and I asked, 'I could have had a child?'

Weeping, she nodded. Then she whispered, 'It gets worse.'

She was fucking kidding. What could be worse? All those years of yearning for a child, I'd actually done the deed and the . . .

I wanted to smash something, to drink the Corrib dry, to be numb.

Sister Maeve's voice softened. 'Siobhans's suicide and the abortion . . . it was like they merged, became one part of a mosaic of horror and loss. And Jo was truly lost. Then she read or heard about the death of Serena May – is that the little girl's name?'

I nodded.

'It was as if that became the catalyst, the fusion of all the trauma, all the terrible events, and gave her a focus. Now she could, as it were, lay it all on one single act. I'm not suggesting this was rational but she was in such a horrendous state of mind, she would have locked on to anything to escape the terror of her own thoughts.'

'Where is she?'

Maeve seemed to have retreated into herself. The awful anguish of what had happened had finally caught up with her and she could no longer even think about it. She stared down at her hands, and I noticed the nails had dug into the palms, drawing blood.

25

Country of the Blind

The country went Lotto mad. A rollover brought it up to sixteen million and tickets were selling at the rate of twenty thousand a minute.

Summer was coming in Irish fashion – teeming rain and lashing storms. By a supreme effort of will, I reined my drinking way in. But I needed help lest I go on a bender again. Next time, I didn't think I'd wake by the canal but in it.

You want to score dope, it's beyond simplicity. Go and sit on Eyre Square, wrestle a bench from a wino or backpacker and wait. Course, you'll also be offered everything else that a city drunk on new money has to offer the not-so-discerning buyer.

My first day, I struck out but did manage to part with some euros to a drinking school who blessed me with *'Bheannacht leat'*, 'Blessings on you'.

Benediction indeed.

I was sitting on the bench the second day, listening to Johnny Duhan's album *Just Another Town*. Been a while since I listened to J.D. as his music reminded me too much of harsher times – the horrendous killing-of-the-tinkers episode and the tragic conclusions I'd reached. Track three kicked in and I nearly jumped; it was titled, 'Benediction'.

How the fuck did I forget that?

Before I could get to listen to the lyrics, a guy in his twenties, with long dank hair, combat trousers and a sweatshirt asked, 'Where were you when John died?'

I looked at him. 'I was in a pub in Donegal, drinking poteen.'

'What?'

Obviously the question had been rhetorical.

He said, 'You looking for something?'

I cut through the shite. 'What have you got?'

He got suspicious, asked, 'You a cop?'

I turned away.

He moved a little closer, went all hippy. 'Hey man, no offence, but like, I gotta watch my back, you hear what I'm saying?'

I was going to snap, 'I'm not deaf.' But I was certainly heading that way.

He said, 'I see you got you a limp there, dude. The citizens putting it to you right?'

I gave him my granite look and he went into the rap. Uppers. Downers. Beauties. Ice. Weed, Colombian Gold.

I put up my hand, said, 'Xanax.'

He let out a long breath. 'Got me some Valium, 10mg . . . chill you right out.'

I gritted my teeth, said, 'If I wanted fucking Valium, you think I wouldn't have said?'

He smiled like a rodent with a plan. 'Heavy vibe, dude. But yeah, I can get you those bad babes. Gonna take like an hour, and gonna cost. You down with that?'

All the Irish youth talked like this now. What a fucking tragedy.

I told him I was indeed *down* with that and told him how many I wanted.

His eyes widened. He stood up and asked, 'You be mellow, I'll be back in, like, warp speed. Anything else you need?'

'Just that you don't call me fucking dude.'

He was striding off and I had to ask, though I doubt he was even born, 'Where were you when John died?'

He looked confused.

'John who?'

Such times, I love the sheer lunacy of my country.

26

Watch the World Slide By

I watched the crowds passing, bemused – not one Galway accent to be heard. It had been on the news that we were the second richest nation behind Japan. There were, at the last count, nearly four thousand millionaires in the state, and yeah, the poor were getting seriously poorer.

A woman, dressed in a shawl, cautiously approached. She was an indeterminate fifty, had the Romanian look, all bangles and rings. The government had recently chartered a flight, made a pre-dawn swoop and gathered up nearly a hundred of these people who were camping on the M1.

Oh yeah, we were rich and getting real ruthless.

A cycling team from Latvia, due to take part in the Round Ireland Race, had if not legged it, certainly disappeared. I couldn't help wondering what they did with the bikes.

She asked in a clipped Brit voice, 'Is this seat free?' That way the Brits have of making everything sound imperious and commanding.

I looked round – lots of vacant benches – but said, 'It's vacant. Very little is free here any more.' Even the public toilets were pay-as-you-go.

She eyed me warily, wondering if she was making a terrible mistake, then sat cautiously down, keeping a safe distance between us. She took out a paper bag jammed with bread-crumbs and I thought, *Uh-oh*. Said, 'If you're going to feed the pigeons, you might want to bear something in mind.'

She paused – mid-crumb, so to speak – and I said, 'Apart from the fact that they are flying rodents, you're just fattening them up. Come evening, the New Age travellers net them and roast them over their campfires down near the pier.'

In that precise, clipped tone she said, 'Surely you jest?'

I turned to face her. 'Jest? Lady I've done lots of stuff in my life, but jesting hasn't yet been one of them.'

Then lo and behold, a perfect single white feather came floating on the slight breeze and landed at our feet.

She was delighted, clapped her hands in joy, asked, 'Do you know what that means?'

Many replies suggested themselves, all sarcastic, e.g. *A bird doesn't fly on one wing.* But I went with 'No.'

I picked it up and it was pristine, almost like the quills the monks used.

She said, 'When a feather floats by, it means your angel is close by.'

Right.

I handed it to her.

She protested, 'Oh no, I couldn't.'

'I insist.'

She took it gently, like a baby, put it delicately in her bag, then took out a card and said, 'This is for you.'

I saw my drug-dealer approach. She stood and said, 'My angel thanks you.'

And in then the brief moment when I should have been paying attention, which of course I wasn't, she added, 'Brian will love that.'

And she was gone.

The guy sat, looked round carefully, then laid an envelope on the bench. I palmed him the money and he said, 'You need a refill, come back to this bench anytime.'

As he stood up I said, 'My angel thanks you.'

He stared at me. 'What?'

I shook my head, said, 'I jest.'

I took the envelope, slipped it casually in my pocket, then remembered the card the pigeon lady had given me. It had a picture of a dark angel with a sword, slashing the bejaysus out of a serpent. I turned it over, and the print on the back said:

> *In benedictus*
> *Requiescat in pace.*

Holy fuck. It was her.

I jumped up, but she was long gone.

Despite the warming sun, I felt a chill run down my spine. Ice cold, like evil has reached out and touched you with its malevolence.

I opened the envelope, took out one of the pills, swallowed it and hoped to Christ they were as good as the character in John Straley's novels claimed. He had described the effect as like being wrapped in cotton wool, a warm woozy feeling.

I stayed sitting, chilled to the depths of my very soul.

I felt powerless, wondering if she was watching me – not a feeling I'm used to. I've always been able to take action – usually of the worst kind, but able to function. This feeling was not only new but scary.

A familiar figure came shambling across the square, enveloped in nicotine. Father Malachy. He looked as he always did: angry, shabby, about to explode. Then his eyes lit on me and he approached.

No warm greeting, just straight in. 'Too drunk to move, Taylor?'

Nice.

I gave him a bitter smile. 'Actually I'm dealing drugs.'

He sat down, wheezing deeply. 'That wouldn't surprise me at all.'

He indicated the drinking school, who knew better than to approach him. 'That's the crowd you belong with and I don't doubt you're soon to join them.'

I asked, 'Do you believe in angels?'

He looked at me, suspicion writ huge. 'Why?'

I could feel a warm mellowness beginning to take hold. God bless pharmaceuticals.

'Well, you're a priest, sort of, and angels and all that stuff is your . . . How should I put it? Your merchandise.'

I saw a slow cunning light his eyes and knew he was ready to retaliate.

He said, 'Your mother was an angel.'

I let him savour that for a bit then said, 'So was Lucifer.'

He blessed himself – not easy with a cigarette in his hand, and ash dribbled on to his black jacket. He said, 'In the name of all that's holy, may God forgive you for that blasphemy.'

He sat in seething silence and I asked, 'If a nun had to hide out, away from the convent, where would she go?'

He was startled. 'What kind of eejit question is that? All I know about nuns is they are great shiners. Nobody can polish a floor like a nun.'

The pill was kicking in big time and I felt almost warm towards it. Jesus, now that is one dynamite medication. I said, 'Useful as that gem of information is, should I just go check out shining floors and follow the trail?'

He was getting fidgety – must be out of cigarettes, though I didn't know how he could afford them now they were over seven euro a pack. But then money was never a problem for the clergy.

He asked, 'Why on God's earth would you want to find a nun?'

I told him the truth. 'Because she's killing people.'

He shook his head – more of my paranoid nonsense. But instead of attacking me he said, 'I did my novitiate in Rome. Ah Lord God, 'twas heaven. Sun, wine . . .' And for a moment, his face relaxed.

I caught a glimpse of a young man, a decent one, who once used to laugh, and not from bitterness.

He shook himself out of the reverie, said, 'The Italians had a saying: "If you ever walk past a nun, touch a piece of iron and say, 'Your nun' to a passer-by – passing any bad luck to them."'

Well, I had iron in my pocket, a revolver, and was touching it right now.

He stood up, looked right at me, some of the Roman decency still lingering, and said, 'You were brought up Catholic and you read all those books and you think you're so smart? So use your head, boyo. Where would a nun hide? She can't go home – the convent is out of bounds.'

And he headed off.

I shouted, 'Where?'

'Use your head, yah eejit.'

My head was full of cotton wool. I couldn't figure it out, and the Xanax whispered, 'Why bother?'

But it was almost a Zen question and there was only one person who could help with that: Stewart.

So I called him, said, 'I need your help.'

A pause. My requests tended to get people hurt and he had the sore head to prove it.

He said, 'Jack, you're forgetting something.'

'That you got hurt already?'

Almost a laugh, then, 'No Jack, the item you're big on yourself – manners. Like, *please*.'

Jesus. I said, 'Please?'

'You sure hate that, Jack, don't you? Come round, I'm near finished my meditation so I should be grounded enough, even for you.'

I clicked off. Was that insulting?

The Xanax answered, 'Who gives a fuck?'

I liked that answer and I loved this drug.

27

Just Another Town

I was due to meet with Stewart that evening
and was amazed I didn't need a drink. The
Xanax had me chilled. I had no illusions that
it too would come with some major price tag.
I'd seen photos of major stars heading for rehab
after – what's the buzz word? – yeah, *dabbling*.
They still looked better than me in all me years
of no booze so I'd pay the chit, as I always did.
But for now, it kept me off the booze and for
that I was, if not grateful, at least relieved.

An added bonus: I could read again. The
hangovers had been getting so bad, I was unable even to do that. So I took a trip down to
Charly Byrnes. Jeez, how long since I'd seen
Vinny? Too long.

He was behind the counter, long dark hair nigh covering his face, as per usual, and telling an old lady, 'You bring the books in, I'll look after you.'

You could tell she didn't give a toss about the books, but Vinny looking after her . . . he had the gift and the thing is, he meant it.

She floated out of the shop.

I said, 'You never lost it.'

He turned. Took him a moment, then, 'Jack! I thought you'd left us, gone to America?'

I went with the familiar. 'Ah, you can't get rid of a bad thing.'

He nodded, a hundred things going on in that mind of his. 'So they keep telling *me*. You up for a coffee?'

I was.

We headed for Quay Street, Vinny expertly sidestepping every

Howyah?
Can you spare us a few euro?
You owe me a pint
You owe me a moment
You look great.

The usual music of a Galway street. He responded to all with affection, never once giving offence, even stopping to put some notes in a busker's cap. The guy shouted, 'I'll buy you a pint later, Vinny.'

He smiled, said to me, 'And that will be the day.'

I envied him, the way he could manoeuvre all this street life and still be loved. Me, I'd have been getting the hurley to half of them.

We went into Café du Journal. How Irish is that? It was packed, but he found a table amid the chaos, said, 'This will do grand.'

And before you could blink, the waitress, a gorgeous non-national, had put an expresso, a slice of Danish and – get this – a folded copy of *The Irish Times* in front of him. She said, 'I'll be back for friend's order.'

He gave that smile that is the reason you get that kind of treatment.

Me, I get barred.

I mention meeting Vinny and this whole brief encounter as it was such an oasis of *normalcy* in my out-of-control life.

What is it they say? A trainwreck waiting to happen. Fuck, I was already flattened by the train and waiting for the express to finish me off.

I asked him, pun intended, I suppose, 'Vinny, you ever get . . . you know . . . derailed?'

He put aside the paper and considered my question. One of the things I loved about him, he never took a query lightly. He sipped at his expresso, then said, 'I watch the signals.'

Does it get any deeper?

And yet stays within the Irish male boundaries of never being too serious, least on the surface.

The waitress returned, again all smiles for Vinny, and asked what I would like. I said a latte would be just great.

Moving on from our moment of seriousness, I said, 'I need to order some books, mate.'

He beamed. 'Music to my ears. The usual blend of crime, poetry and philosophy?'

I said that would do the job and we chatted about nothing and everything, staying light, staying Irish.

He told me he'd been to a concert by Philip Fogarty and Anna Lardi in Saint Nicholas's Church and I feigned horror. 'A Protestant Church? You're fucked.'

He laughed, a real deep-down-in-the-stomach, heart-warming one. 'Well, I had me rosary beads with me.'

I smiled, a strange feeling, said, 'Naw, you're screwed.'

We'd finished the coffee. Time to go.

Outside, he warded off the usual well-wishers and I said, 'So the concert, you heathen, was it good?'

He gave a few euro to a wino. 'It was brilliant. That Philip, he sure can work the crowd, and Anna . . . poetry in song.' Then he added, 'If I say 'twas a guilty pleasure, will I earn back some points from the man above?'

I acted like I was thinking about it, then said, 'Actually makes it worse. Better climb Croagh Patrick.'

'Barefoot?'

'Is there any other way?'

He laughed again and was gone.

The pilgrims climb Croagh Patrick in Mayo every year and it's a steep rocky haul. The rescue services always have to airlift some poor bastard who's had a heart attack, or suffered dehydration, and on top of the mountain is the Statue of Saint Patrick. I wondered whether, with all the snakes we had in our society at the moment, he was as alert as he once was. Losing his grip, like all the other icons, heroes we once adored.

They should get real honest and put the euro sign up there and then they wouldn't climb the mountain, they'd fucking gallop. Barefoot or not.

28

Dark Proposal

I was en route to meet Stewart when my mobile rang. I dreaded and hoped it might be the psycho nun.

I heard a cultured male voice. 'Mr Taylor, I do pray I haven't caught you at a bad time?'

The Anglo-Irish prick. As I tried to resurrect his name, he supplied it: 'Anthony Bradford-Hemple here. I trust you remember me?'

'Sure, Hemple, I remember.'

A slight intake of breath at my obvious rudeness. What did he expect? *Mr? Sir?*

He composed himself and said, 'One tends to forget the somewhat acidic nature of your tongue, Mr Taylor. I have been rather remiss in not expressing my gratitude for your colleague's splendid work on behalf of my daughter.'

Colleague?

Ridge.

I said, with the same edge in my voice, 'Glad to be of help.'

'I wanted to tell you how happy I am, and really, it's all down to you. I'd never have had the sheer audacity to hope again, and now with Cathleen I'm rather dizzy with delight.'

Who the fuck was Cathleen? Without thinking, I echoed meself with 'Who the fuck is Cathleen?'

He gave what the Brits call a 'hearty chuckle' and said, 'Oh, do forgive me. She is probably more formal with you. I mean, of course, Ban Garda Ridge.'

What the hell was he talking about? Was he hitting the port big time? I asked, 'What are you on about?

He gave a milder form of the previous chuckle, just as annoying. 'Oh dear, I fear I may have jumped the gun. I presumed she'd have told you.'

'Told me what?'

I swear, a triumphant note in his tone now. 'I daresay I'd better let Cathleen spill the beans . . . Not really my place. Anyway, on Friday we're having a little soirée to celebrate at my modest pile and would dearly love to have you in attendance. Nothing too formal, tie and blazer would be more than adequate.'

And he hung up.

I was standing in the middle of Shop Street by this stage, buskers to the right of me, mimers to the left, and I felt I'd wandered into a circus. The phone rang again. I was ready for him this time and was about to launch when I heard a woman's voice.

'You were so kind to give me the feather.'

I was too stunned to answer.

She continued, 'I have the child and soon it will be your turn, Mr Taylor – or should I call you Jack?'

There was no malice or rage in her voice, which made it all the more chilling. More like she was telling me the shopping list was nigh done.

I said, 'You psycho bitch, I'll get you if it's the last thing I do.'

She made a sound – a laugh, a sigh, I don't know. 'No truer words, Mr Taylor. It will be the last thing you do. Alas, I had to smite my sinner brother for yet one more betrayal. It's on your head, Mr Taylor, as is so much. But you have so very little time left in which to be a plague on what was once holy ground.'

And she was gone.

What the hell did she mean?

I felt a shock of fear to my whole system. She had taken a child. Which child? Jesus, I had to find out and quickly. Which meant I needed to get round to see her brother without delay.

29

My Brother's Keeper?

As I ran to meet Stewart, the skies darkened.
Who was it – Eliot? – who wrote something
about what the thunder said. In Galway it said,
'You're fucked.'

Stewart was all settled in for a chat and tea. I
grabbed his arm. 'We have to move and fast.'

Probably didn't fit in with his Zen gig but
I wasn't in the mood for any laid-back bullshit and as I steered him towards Ben's house
– I couldn't call him Benedict – I told him all
the stuff that had gone down. Meeting with
the psycho nun's brother, then her giving me
the feather, her call . . . and her ominous final
warning about what had happened to her
brother for his 'betrayal'.

We'd reached the Fair Green by now, not a spit away from the church where the priest had been decapitated. This had been the case where Father Malachy had enlisted my help to try and find whoever had killed the priest. I'd like to say it had turned out well. It hadn't.

Stewart stopped. 'Phew, slow down. Let me digest some of this.'

Digest?

I said, 'We're not having fucking lunch, we're trying to see if a poor bastard needs help.'

He still wasn't moving. I wanted to wallop him, hard.

He asked in that ultra-cool tone, 'So why didn't you call Ridge? You want her back in action.'

I said through gritted teeth, 'Because it looks like she's making marriage plans.'

That finally got a stir out of him. He nearly gasped. 'Wow! Who's the lucky woman?'

How much had we changed in our society that he naturally presumed it was a woman. I know he knew Ridge was gay, but the ease with which he asked was still startling.

I said, 'Look, can we do all this shite later?'

He finally moved, said, 'Jack, don't you ever wish for a more . . . uneventful life?'

I could have gone deep and said, *I wish for some peace*. Like that was going to happen. I went with 'I wish you'd shut the fuck up.'

He did.

We got to the house and the door opened at our touch.

I said, 'I'll go first.'

He nearly smiled. 'That's why we pay you the big bucks.'

We found him upstairs in bed. He looked terrible.

He said, 'Jack, my constant visitor, you've arrived with little time to spare. My sister was here and persuaded me to have a drink.'

His smile was almost beatific in its glow. He continued, 'I'm always up for a drink – I'm sure you can empathize. But she had laced it with some kind of poison, not too painful but deadly . . . I can feel my life pouring away and it seems sort of fitting that you should be the witness to my demise.'

'I'll call an ambulance.'

He shook his head. 'Have one for the road with me, Jack. A drink, that is, not an ambulance.'

He gave a small laugh at his wit and it caused

a horrendous bout of coughing. He managed to gasp, 'God in heaven, I'm glad I never smoked.'

I had, alas, seen enough men die to know he was right. Already that waxen pallor had circled his face.

There was a bottle of Bushmills on the dresser and some glasses. I poured two large ones, handed one to him.

He studied the glass as if it might tell him something.

'What shall we drink to, Jack?'

Jesus wept.

Long life?

He said, 'Let's toast the friendship we might have had.'

We clinked glasses and drank deep.

I felt such a wave of affection for this man. I didn't try to figure why, it was just instinct.

We heard Stewart climbing the stairs.

Stewart, on seeing the colour of the man, looked like he was going to throw up. So much for fucking Zen.

Benedict said, 'There's some nice iced water in the fridge downstairs if you feel faint.'

Jesus, I couldn't help but like this poor sad bastard. He was unable to move because of his sheer girth and he still had fucking manners. That killed me, and I swore an oath, an unholy one, that I'd make that bitch suffer as I killed her.

He said, 'Jack, it's OK, I don't mind shuffling off this mortal coil, if you'll excuse my showing off my little learning. And as they say in the Claddagh, "Death was a blessed relief."'

I have never hugged another man, not even me own beloved father. It's our upbringing – you never put your hand on another man unless you want to lose it from the shoulder. Now I leaned over and put me two arms round this massive man.

He started to cry, muttered, 'Thanks, Jack.'

Fuck, fuck and fuck it all.

This hugely obese man, lonely as only the truly lost can be, was thanking me and he wouldn't let go. I had the horrendous thought, *He's never had a hug in his whole life.* And that the first should have to be from a fucked, deaf, limping trainwreck like me . . .

God is in his heaven and I had some serious issues to run by him.

I clapped Benedict's back, lied, 'It's going to be all right.'

No – that it certainly wasn't. But it would be

fucking medieval when I caught up with her.

We, how do you say, disentangled, and he said, 'I needed that.'

Then he looked at me – I mean, truly saw me – and said, 'There is a goodness in you, Jack. You deny it, fight it and act like you don't care in every way you can. Is it self-preservation that makes you go hard arse against the world? But you know something? . . . Jack . . . I love you.'

Then he closed his eyes and died . . . right there in front of me.

I touched his face, rubbed his massive cheek and said, 'I wish I could have been your friend.'

God only knows what he'd endured in his life. I could only guess. I pulled the sheet up over his huge body and touched his hand. It was still warm. I squeezed it and said, 'You were a gentle man.'

And the fucking rage in me . . . I'd been angry, enraged and all that, but this was a whole new era.

Stewart returned with a bottle of Galway bottled water and I took it to wash down a Xanax. Stewart didn't comment, just looked at the sheet pulled up.

I said, 'He's dead.'

Stewart seemed mesmerized by the sheer size of the poor bastard. He said, 'He sure was—'

I grabbed his arm. 'You use the word *fat* and I'll break your fucking arm.'

He pulled his arm free. 'I was going to say *brave*.'

Then he asked, 'What are we going to do?'

The only thing to do.

'Get the hell out of here.'

'Shouldn't we call someone?'

As I headed down the stairs, sick to my very stomach, I said, 'It's a little late for the Samaritans.'

30

Dead Eyes

We went into the Park Hotel and sat in the lounge. A waitress arrived, all smiles – not Irish, of course, no one in the service industry is any more – and asked what we'd like. I ordered a large cola and Jesus, did I need that sugar rush. Stewart said he'd have a sparkling water, ice and lemon, please.

He looked at me. 'Not drinking?'

I couldn't get the eyes of the dead man out of my mind. 'Not yet anyway.'

The drinks came and Stewart said, 'My treat.'

Made my fucking day.

I gulped down the cola and winced at the sheer amount of sugar I could taste.

Stewart raised an eyebrow. 'Bit sweet for you, Jack?'

I snapped, 'I don't do sweet.'

'Really?'

Neither of us was ready to discuss what we'd seen or what'd happened back there.

I got back to my to my apartment and opened the door. Worry about the child was literally gnawing at me guts, and I felt a foreboding unlike any I'd experienced. I turned on the light and got one of the hardest wallops to my jaw I've had, and God knows I've had me share.

That knocked me back against the door frame and then an almighty kick to the balls had me throw up whatever shite was in me system.

When my vision cleared and the pain in my groin had eased a little, I managed to see two hard-arsed guards – the shoes are how you know the fucks – and sitting in me only comfortable chair was Clancy.

He hissed, 'Where's my boy?'

I muttered, 'What?'

'Brian, my two-year-old son.'

Oh sweet Jesus, when the nun had sat on the bench with me she'd said, *'and Brian thanks you.*' She was literally telling me whose son she was taking. God almighty, she'd taken Clancy's!

The two guards with him were big and ready for action, like pit bulls straining against the leash, and I knew the leash was about to be unfastened. One of them, in his bad fifties, had a scar along his right cheek, testament to lots of action. The other held one of those new plastic batons, lightweight and oh so flexible. Don't let the term 'plastic' mislead you – they are deadly, inflict pain that is as harsh as it is rapid, and joy of joys, they don't leave marks, not ones you could show to a lawyer. He was tapping it absent-mindedly against his right hand, his eyes fixed on me, just waiting to use it.

I tested my legs and tried to stand.

Clancy spat, 'Did I tell you to get up?'

My mouth, always my downfall, came out with 'No, I'm a mind-reader.'

I received a ferocious lash of the baton across the bridge of my nose.

Clancy had a bottle of Jameson by his chair. No glass, which was a bad sign. The boyos, in the bad old days, when they intended serious damage always brought a bottle, no glasses. You saw that, you were in for a long night.

Clancy and I, in our young days when we served on the border, had seen the results of just such evenings and pretty it wasn't.

He took a hefty swig of it now, and his cheeks were almost instantly inflamed. I'd have given my whole cache of Xanax for it.

'Like a shot of this, would you, Jack? Tell you what, you tell me where to find my son and you can have a whole bottle to yourself.'

I said, 'I'm not drinking.'

The two guards were highly amused at that, and Clancy said, 'By Christ, you'll wish you were.'

He nodded at Scar Face. 'This is Tom, hails from Kilkenny, and as you know, they sure produce some fine hurlers. And Old Tom here, he hates guards gone bad. And is there any guard who ever went as rogue as you, Jack?'

I'd have been happier with him addressing me as Taylor. I'd witnessed enough vicious beatings to know that when your Christian name is used, you're seriously fucked. It's part of the psychology, keeps it nice and brutal and, above all, keeps it real personal.

Clancy, indicating with the bottle, said, 'Tom, he's a specialist in – I think you might recall the term, "softening up" a witness and I have to say, he's especially keen to soften up a hard case like your good self.'

I put up a hand, and to my shame it was shaking. I said, 'You can call him off, there's no need, I'll tell you everything I know. I want to help, and I can.'

Clancy smiled malevolently. 'Jack, you're not paying attention. But then, you never did. See, thing is, I've promised Tom a crack at you and trust me – will you trust me, Jack? – after he has his little way with you, you'll sing like a fucking canary.'

Before I could mutter another word, Tom kicked me in the mouth, then proceeded to soften me up. Didn't take long – with a pro it never does. Finally, breathing deeply, he stepped back, sweat on his face, and Clancy said, 'Good man, Tom. That will do for the moment.'

For the moment? Few scarier threats in the whole session.

I've had beatings with hammers, hurleys, boots, fists, and one memorable time with an iron bar, but this particular one took the Oscar. I hurt in ways it didn't seem possible to hurt.

Clancy said, 'This is where the heavy usually says, "I take no pleasure in this."' Then he laughed, a bitter low sound. 'Bollocks, I haven't enjoyed anything as much since Galway won the All Ireland. Think it calls for a minor celebration.'

He reached in his jacket, took out a fat cigar and asked, 'Mind if I smoke, Jack?' He bit the end off and spat it on the floor. 'Whoops.' Then he lit it slowly, savouring the moment, and blew a perfect ring at the ceiling. 'You take a second there, Jack, compose yourself, and then we'll talk. Or should I say, you'll talk.'

Five minutes passed and I heard a church bell ring, probably from the Claddagh. I remembered in my youth when a church bell rang, people would stop and say the Angelus. I couldn't even recall the words any more, and I must have recited it every day for years.

Clancy, half the cigar gone, put the rest under his shoe and ground it to shreds, his vehemence apparent in the force of the gesture. He looked at me and said, 'Talk.'

I did.

With a great deal of effort. Every part of me was howling in agony, as if each word cut a fresh pain in my being. I told him about the letter at the very beginning and didn't say, *I tried to tell you twice before about this.* I just continued on. The only thing I left out was the death of the psycho nun's brother. He'd discover that soon enough. I did say she had a brother but said I believed she had no love for him either.

When I was done, he said, 'Describe her.'

I gave it my best shot.

He considered that, then asked, 'So why, Mr Amazing Private Dick, haven't you been able to find her?'

'I don't know.'

For a moment it looked like he was going to unleash Tom again. Then he said, 'I'll tell you why. Because you're a fuck up. Now I'm putting every available man on this, but you, Taylor, are going to get your fucking act together and find her. If any harm comes to my son . . .'

And here he had to pause, as if something was lodged in his throat. Then he shook it off and continued, 'If one bloody hair on his head is harmed, you're going in the river, and that's a promise.'

He stood up, straightened his clothes, looked round and said, 'And clean this place up. It's a fucking pigsty.'

When they were gone, I crawled over to the bureau, pulled out the drawer and swallowed two Xanax. The bottle of Jameson was lying on the floor beside the chair Clancy had been sitting in, and there was perhaps one decent glassful remaining. I turned away, got my mobile out of my jacket. I was surprised it still worked after Tom's efforts. I tried to hit the buttons but my eyes kept blurring. Finally I heard it ring and a voice said, 'Yes?'

'Stewart, I need your help. Could you come to my place?'

'Are you hurt?'

I'd have laughed but knew it would hurt too much. I said, 'I've been better.'

And passed out.

31

Sanctuary

I don't remember much about the next forty-eight hours. Stewart had brought a concoction of Chinese remedies and medications and I think I said, 'I'm not drinking any fucking herbal tea.'

He may have laughed.

I do know he applied various lotions to my body and I said, 'Hope you're not getting off on this.'

His smiled grimly. 'Jack, you seen your body lately? Trust me, not even medical science would have an interest.'

I drifted in and out of consciousness, Stewart feeding me soup and potions. As he coerced me to drink some foul liquid he said, 'This will knock you out.'

I might be able to pass it on to the guard, Tom, to save him kicking the shite out of people. I thought I kept hearing bells, though maybe they were just ringing in my head from the beating. But something was lurking on the edge of my mind and I couldn't quite grasp hold of it.

When I was finally able to sit up, feel the beating receding, Stewart said, 'You're looking better. How do you feel?'

'Hungry.'

He was about to reach into his bag of tricks and I said, 'Fuck, no. Enough with the eastern stuff. I need some real food, like a fry-up.'

He sighed. 'That crap will clog your arteries.'

I laughed and it didn't hurt too much. 'Stewart, look at me. You really think a few sausages and fried eggs are going to make a whole lot of difference to my general well-being?'

He nodded then asked, 'What's with the Ave Marias?'

'What?'

He was laying out some clean clothes and

I was afraid to ask if he'd done me laundry. He said, 'You kept crying out "Its sweet tones announcing the sacred *ave*" and other variations along those lines.'

The Angelus.

I said, 'Oh fuck.'

He shook his head. 'Sounds more like the Jack we know.'

I stood up. Despite a slight dizziness, I was OK. 'The Angelus – it's been obsessing me all this time. Don't you see what it means?'

He didn't. 'You're getting religious?'

My mind was clearing and I said, 'Where would a nun feel safe, seek shelter – seek sanctuary, so to speak – apart from a convent? Where would she be warm and, best of all, familiar?'

He shook his head.

'She's hiding out in a church,' I told him.

He thought about it. 'Makes sense. Galway might be cosmopolitan but we still have a lot of churches – nearly as many as pubs.'

I found a sheet of paper and started to list all the churches. 'She'd have to use one that is familiar to her, where she knows the routine of the priests, when it's safe to be there, and one she has access to.'

Stewart said, 'I could ring the Mother Superior, ask what church they used.'

'But convents have their own churches. She's hardly using that.'

He grabbed the piece of paper, looked at the list, said he'd make a few calls.

I used the time to have a shower and managed to wash without seeing too much of the markings on my body. The plastic baton mightn't leave signs but fists and boots sure do. But I was energized, I could feel the hunt in my blood and knew it was coming to the final showdown. I had a flash of intuition: why had Benedictus killed the nun? Of course, they'd thrown her out of the order, she'd been betrayed by her own, and so one of them had to atone for that.

When I got out of the shower, I had a blast of pure instinct and asked Stewart, 'May I use your laptop?'

'Sure.'

The adrenalin was shooting through my veins and I knew I was on course. I hit Google and typed in my request.

A moment, then up it came.

I muttered, 'Jesus . . . I was right.'

It was so obvious when you did the math.

Stewart said, 'The Mother Superior asked me to high tea when I called her.'

'There's a low one?'

He smirked, said, 'Yeah, for the Jack Taylors of this world.'

I let that slide. 'Sounds like you're a real hit with the Mother Superior.'

'I could say I've a way with nuns but that sounds off.'

Not these days, if the papers were any indication.

He jabbed his finger on the sheet of paper, said, 'Two churches, Salthill and the cathedral. The Mother Superior told me that their order was responsible for those two churches.'

I lied, 'Salthill sounds the most likely.'

'Why?'

I kept my face in neutral, said, 'Rich parish, they can afford the heating.'

I knew something Stewart didn't. The cathedral had a basement. I was tempted to tell him they kept the bodies of the bishops there and where better to hide a child? But instinct told me to keep that to myself.

Stewart hesitated then asked, 'Jack, I hate to mention it, but how do we know the child is still alive? Wouldn't she have, you know, done the deed by now? It's been nearly five days.'

He told me the guards had literally blanket-ed the town, raiding every conceivable hiding place, rousing touts, leaning on snitches. The whole force was involved in the search.

I said, 'She's waiting for me before she kills the child. She needs me as a witness. Don't ask me why, but that seems to be part of her warped plan.'

'And Jack, what is your warped plan?'

I said, 'We check out the two places ourselves first. I don't want to bring the cops over on a wild goose chase, based purely on a hunch.'

'So we go over to Salthill tonight? I'm pre-suming night is the time to go as the church should be closed then and we can operate with-out prying eyes.'

He was almost right. I said, 'Night, yes, and Salthill first. Bring Ridge. Give her career a real boost if we're right.'

He was suspicious. 'What about you?'

I trod real careful, said, 'I'll check out the cathedral and then head out to Salthill. This way we cover all our bases and save time.'

He gave me a long look. 'There's something off about this, Jack. Are you telling me every-thing?'

I had to distract him. I raised my voice, said, 'What's off is the crazy bitch has a child and we can't afford to be wrong.'

He wasn't fully buying it, but went along with it.

I said, 'Breakfast, my treat. And hey, you can even have herbal tea.'

As we headed out, he grumbled, 'I could have had high tea.'

If I didn't know better, I might have thought Stewart was developing a sense of humour.

32

Little Boy Lost

For breakfast, I ordered:

> Three sausages
> Two fried eggs
> Black pudding
> Fried tomatoes
> Toast
> A pot of coffee

Stewart asked for a muffin and decaffeinated tea.

The waitress, in her fifties, went, 'What?'

She was that rarity, Irish, and so still spoke to customers. The café was one of the nigh-on-extinct breed, hidden off a small street near the Jesuit School. You knew it was old style as it was crammed with guys from the building trade, more than usual for that time of day – the building game, like everything else, was in meltdown. Mortgages had gone through the roof, so to speak, and first-time buyers were seriously screwed. The waitress had heard just about everything, but decaffeinated tea?

She looked at me, asked, 'Is he codding me?'

Her face was vaguely familiar, but then anyone Irish looked familiar these days as there seemed to be so few.

I said, 'He's young.'

She looked at him. 'Well, he's certainly in the wrong place.'

Stewart was smart and said nothing

I suggested she squeeze the hell out of the tea bag and she enjoyed that. She said, 'Just what I need on my busiest shift, squeezing the life out of a tea bag.'

I could hear snatches of conversation and for once it wasn't about the water, it was about Clancy's boy. Neither the papers or the guards had released any details about the ex-nun: the clergy were in enough strife. But a backlash had already begun. A well-known paedophile, recently released, had had his home burnt out and dark mutterings could be heard about various perverts being run out of town.

Stewart asked, 'Have you seen your old . . . er . . . friend Jeff recently?'

I hadn't.

Stewart toyed with his cutlery, then said, 'His wife, Cathy . . . she's back in town. I think they may be attempting to get back together.'

'Lucky them.' Bitterness leaking all over my tone.

He was quiet for a time, then said, 'What are you going to do, Jack?'

Jesus, I had an overwhelming desire for a cigarette. I contemplated going outside to where a bunch of smokers were huddled and bumming one.

'About what?'

He sighed. 'You know what I mean.'

I did.

I said, 'Let's get that little boy back first.'

He wasn't ready to let it go. 'Jack, the woman was sick. Can't you factor that into the mix?'

I could feel anger rising. 'You talking about the fucking nun or the bitch who killed her own child?'

He was about to protest when I added, 'She let me carry the weight for the death of Ser—'

Still couldn't say her name. 'The child. All that guilt, and what came after . . . some things are unforgivable.'

He stared into my eyes, then said, 'Jack, you of all people might want to reconsider that.'

I was spared a reply and just as well, as it would have been ugly.

The waitress brought the food and cautioned, 'Careful, the plate is hot.' She looked at Stewart. 'Not you. We don't put *muffins* on heated plates.'

Stewart looked at my pile of cholesterol and simply shook his head.

I said, 'Call it comfort food.'

The waitress returned with my coffee and the tea and plonked them down. She said, 'Enjoy' to me and, to Stewart, 'Endure.'

We both looked at the tea bag. It seemed to have been put through the wringer – maybe it had.

I said, 'Guess she got all the caffeine out of there.'

He pushed it aside. 'And everything else.'

I ate with relish. Stewart made a grimace as I forked some black pudding and dipped it in the runny egg. He said, 'How can you eat that?' Meaning the black pudding.

'The late Pope on his visit here liked it a lot.'

'Might explain why he's the *late* Pope.'

As we were leaving, I said, 'My treat.'

Stewart replied, 'My cup runneth over, de-caff or otherwise.'

Like I said, he was definitely getting the hang of the humour biz.

I left him outside the café, saying I'd see him around ten or so that evening at the Salthill church. He was turning to leave when I suggested he might consider bringing something to protect himself.

He said, 'I have my martial arts.'

I thought maybe I should shake his hand or something, but went with 'You'll fucking need them.'

I went shopping. I had a list of items I figured I'd need. You're going to stake out a church, it could be a long wait. Top of the list was a decent torch; the rest of the stuff I managed to get within an hour.

I walked slowly back to my place, all sorts of ideas screaming through my head, mainly the terrible thought that I might not be able to save the child. Oh sweet Jesus, I would not be able to lose another child.

A woman was selling pins for charity on

the corner of Dominic Street and, talk about irony, the pins were tiny angels in aid of abused children. Into my head unbidden came the Irish term *Angeail an Dorchadas* . . . Angel of Darkness.

I gave a few euro to the seller, but didn't wait to receive the pin.

Back at my flat, I rang the cathedral and asked what time confessions were finished. I wanted a place to hide before they locked up for the night, and on hearing five in the afternoon, asked, 'Any evening devotions?'

The woman, a nun perhaps, said, 'You mean Benediction?'

I felt a tiny finger of ice creep along my spine.

Jesus.

I said, 'Yes.'

She had a warm voice, but it didn't do much for the chill I was feeling. She said, 'No dear, Benediction is on Tuesday and Thursday.'

I thanked her for her help and she added, 'You're welcome. God bless you.'

Christ, someone would need to.

33

Confession Is Good
for the Soul

I got to the cathedral early, my holdall containing my essentials. I took a look around and slipped into the confessional.

It was comfortable and warm, but no, I'm not going to call it a place of sanctuary. Not for me anyway.

I settled down to wait.

I must have dozed off and woke with a start. I checked my watch. Jesus, ten-thirty in the evening. The church had been locked up.

As I emerged from the confessional, the only light was from the eternal candles.

I ate a granola bar and two Xanax, washed down with water. I made me way down the aisle, then came to the door leading to the crypt. My heart was in my mouth. I opened the door carefully and descended the stairs. I didn't need the torch as down below, hundreds of candles were alight.

The crypt was small and claustrophobic, and in the corner lay a tiny bundle. I approached, pulled back the blanket and there was the sleeping child. No sign of harm . . . yet.

And then came the voice, from behind me. 'The antichrist has arrived.'

I turned to face her. She was wearing a nun's habit and holding a long, lethal blade. Her eyes were lit by pure malignancy.

She asked, 'How did you know the child would still be alive?'

Her body was poised to strike, candlelight bouncing off the wicked-looking blade.

I positioned myself between her and the child and said, 'Today is the anniversary of your sister's suicide.' I'd checked it out on Stewart's laptop.

She gave what might have been construed as a slight smile but was more in the zone of rictus.

I added, 'I'm taking this child out of here and I strongly advise you against trying to stop me.'

She moved closer, the blade coming up, and asked, in a sing-song voice, 'How are you going to do that?'

I produced the revolver, pulled back the hammer.

She lunged and I pulled the trigger.

Nothing.

Would you fucking believe it? It jammed.

And the blade went into my upper thigh, once, twice, three times, and I crumpled to my knees, the useless revolver skittering across the marble floor like so many unheard prayers.

She stood over me, triumph writ huge, and said, 'Prepare to burn for all eternity.'

Her head turned for a moment and whatever voice she was hearing, I knew it wasn't pleading my case.

And I did. I had so many sins to atone for, eternity was not going to be long enough. But as I waited for the final blow, I heard, 'Back off, you crazy bitch.'

Ridge.

And Stewart.

Benedictus didn't even turn, just picked up a heavy candlestick and, whirling, caught Ridge with it on the side of the head.

Stewart moved forward. I hoped to Christ he still had those Zen moves.

Benedictus smiled. 'The third demon.'

She lunged with the blade but Stewart side-stepped, caught her on the back foot and moved in real close to her, as if he was embracing her. She emitted a deep groan, then slowly fell to the ground. I could see one of Stewart's knives, and remembered the seven he'd shown me. It was lodged deep in her chest. Her eyes were wide in astonishment, and then she let out a small sigh and was still.

I was trying to rise up, the pain like acid on my thighs. I asked, 'Did you have to do that?

He looked at me, his eyes sad. 'It was a kind-ness to her. She is no longer in torment.'

Ridge, her eyes groggy, moved to the sleep-ing child, gathered him up and said, 'Let's get the hell out of here. This place gives me the creeps.'

Stewart applied a makeshift tourniquet to my wounds and helped me hobble out.

I asked, 'What about your knife?'

His expression unreadable, he said, 'I still have six.'

I noticed he was wearing gloves.

*   *   *

I was drifting in and out of consciousness and next thing I knew, I was sitting in the armchair of my apartment, Stewart holding out my mobile. He said, 'Don't you have to make a call?'

Clancy answered on the very first ring.

I said, 'I have your boy. He's safe and well.'

His sigh of relief made me almost feel for him again and I swear, he sounded like he had a sob in his voice, as if he was about to break down. But he reined it in, and then with the old tone of command asked where I was and I knew he'd be there immediately.

As Ridge and Stewart prepared to leave, Stewart handed me the useless revolver.

'You forgot this.'

And they were gone.

34

The Guards

Clancy arrived almost on their heels, with his two heavies in tow. Before he could say anything, I handed him the sleeping bundle. 'The crazy nun had your boy sedated, but I don't think he'll suffer any ill effects.'

Clancy's face as he took his child in his arms was something to see. All the hard-arse pose, the mask of ferocity he wore, just slipped away and I nearly felt for him.

I told him that Ridge had put the puzzle together so we were able to track down the psycho.

He asked, in a very quiet voice, 'Where is she now, the woman who kidnapped my boy?'

I told him how she'd nearly got the upper

hand but Ridge had grappled with her and the nun had been stabbed in the struggle. I said he'd find her in the crypt of the church. I wanted Ridge to get the credit – recovering the Chief's child, serious kudos there. He knew there were gaping holes in my account but he had his child back and was prepared to let the inconsistencies slide.

He said, 'I suppose I owe you.'

Blood was seeping through the makeshift tourniquet and he asked, 'You want me to have one of my men drive you to the hospital?'

I shrugged it off and he was silent again.

Then he said, 'Thanks.'

Cost him. He had to dredge it up past all his feelings for me and it near choked him.

I said, 'There is one thing.'

He was still cradling his child in his arms, as if he'd never let go. His two heavies looked slightly uncomfortable. Seeing their boss vulnerable was not something they knew how to cope with.

I said, 'I'd like a moment alone with Tom.'

Tom – who'd beaten me black and blue.

Clancy looked at Tom, who seemed delighted. Another crack at me, maybe? Tom smiled and Clancy said, 'OK.'

He told the other heavy to get a squad together, get over to the church and pick up the
dead nun.

He moved to the door, stopped, was about
to say something, then simply nodded and was
gone.

I was sitting in the armchair, blood still
seeping from my wounds as Tom approached,
flexing his fingers. He asked, 'So Taylor, you
think you're some kind of hero, that it? You're
still shite to me. You got lucky – big deal. You're
the crap I wipe off me shoes.'

I kept my voice low, asked, 'Would you ease
the binding on my leg? I can't reach it.'

He laughed. 'What am I, your fucking
nurse?'

'I think your boss would appreciate you helping me out, just this once.'

He sighed. 'Once . . . and that's it, then the
sheet is clean.'

As he bent down I swung the revolver and
broke his nose. I swung again and broke his
cheekbone. He fell back in pain and astonishment. I levelled the revolver and said, 'Get out
of my home, you bollix.'

He staggered to his feet, wiping the blood
from his face. He looked like he was going to

come at me. I cocked the trigger. We both heard that ominous click as a round slipped into the chamber and I asked, 'Would I shoot you? What do you think?'

He glared at me, said, 'There'll be other times, Taylor.'

I smiled. 'I sure hope so. Now get the fuck out of my house.'

He paused at the door. 'You'd better keep the piece of junk real close, else I'll make you eat it.'

I said, 'Next time, buddy, I'll have a hurley.'

35

Amen

I hate being indebted. Ridge had been instrumental in saving my life and that pissed me off. I know, I should have been down on me knees, thanking her and Stewart for their intervention. But in the back of my mind was the thought, *If there's saving to be done, I'll be the saviour.*

I met with her for coffee a few days later, in Java's on Lower Abbeygate Street. The aroma of real coffee there is like a balm. I got there first, bagged a table at the rear, away from the maddening crowds. In Galway now, there were always crowds. I ordered a double expresso. I'd taken a Xanax earlier and was reasonably chilled; not mellow, but down a notch. Clancy had managed to keep a lid on the return of his son – it wasn't headlined. The nun's body hadn't been found. But I'd seen Stewart put the knife in and saw her face when she fell. She was dead – so who'd taken the body? Not my problem. The church has ways of covering up that would make the Guards seem like amateurs.

Ridge arrived, looking terrific in a new white raincoat, navy top and faded blue jeans. Her hair was just washed and smelt of everything fresh. She gave me a warm smile and ordered a latte.

I said, 'You look well.'

The usual cloud of combat surrounding her was absent.

She said, 'I feel well.'

She'd not only been brought back into the Force, but promotion was coming.

I asked, 'Is it true you're getting married?'

I still couldn't get my head round that.

She took a sip of the latte then said, 'Yes. Anthony is a fine man.'

'But you're gay.'

She didn't get angry, or even raise her voice. 'It's good for my career to be married and Anthony is looking for a companion, more than anything else. And Jennifer, his daughter, is delighted to have a step-mum.'

All so fucking hunky-dory.

'Isn't it a little . . . hypocritical?'

She looked right at me. 'Jack, I have one breast, I'm gay, you think I'm going to be flooded with offers?'

'Isn't marriage sort of outmoded these days? I mean, have you seen the divorce figures?'

She shook her head. 'No matter what you hear, every woman wants to get married. At least, I do – I certainly don't want to end up alone.'

Like you.

The implication hung there.

She broke the ensuing silence with 'I need a favour, Jack.'

See? Already the frigging debt was being called in.

'Spit it out.'

She took a deep breath. 'Will you give me away?'

Ah Jesus.

I said, 'That's your father's gig.'

'He's dead.'

Christ, I'd forgotten.

I was going to ask if there was someone

else . . . God, anybody else, when she said, 'We've had our ups and downs, but nobody really knows me better.'

'OK.'

She smiled. 'Come on, Jack, you might even have fun.'

Right.

She reached in her handbag, produced a ticket and put it on the table. 'This is from Stewart and me. It's for after the wedding.'

I opened it – a ticket to New York.

'You trying to get rid of me?'

She stood up, looked at me, shook her head. 'You will stay sober, won't you, Jack?'

I nodded and she leaned over, and for the first time in all our battered history she gave me a hug.

'Don't be so gloomy, Jack. You'll love America.'

And then she was gone. And I swear to God, she had a spring in her step.

I paid the bill and went outside, and I couldn't believe it, a single white feather was lying on the ground. As I bent to pick it up, a heavy shoe stood on it, mangling it.

I looked up to see Father Malachy, cigarette

in place. I was going to lash him for the feather but figured, one way or another, the Church crushed anything outside their control.

He said, 'Taylor, if you hurry you'll see that mother of the child. She's with your mate, Jeff? Looks like they were shopping in Dunne's and are just now on Shop Street.'

He noticed the feather, which had attached itself to his shoe, and he swore. 'What's this rubbish?'

I said, 'That, Father, is a defeated miracle.'

I hurried along to Shop Street and walked straight into Jeff and Cathy, holding hands. This woman, who'd killed her own child, had given me years of grief and guilt. They halted as I stood before them and I swear, she moved behind Jeff for protection.

I'd envisaged this moment a hundred times and all the various ways I'd make her suffer for my pain. Jeff's eyes pleaded with me.

I said, 'Nice day for it.'

And walked on.

THE END

Also by

KEN
BRUEN

PRIEST

Fresh out of hospital, a new life beckons for troubled **PI Jack Taylor**.

Then Father Joyce is decapitated in a Galway church,
and Taylor is asked to find his killer.

Soon he is drawn into a dark web of murderous conspiracies.

What he cannot know is that the real danger is much closer
and far more personal than he can imagine …

'Hardboiled in the best way, unforgiving and unforgettable'
Sunday Tribune

9780552153430

CROSS

A boy has been crucified in Galway city.

People are shocked; the Irish Church is scandalised.
No further action is taken.

When the sister of the murdered boy is burned alive,
PI Jack Taylor decides to take matters into his own hands.

Taylor's investigations take him to some old city haunts where he
encounters ghosts – living and dead. But what he eventually finds
surpasses even his darkest imaginings…

'A gripping story of guilt and redemption'
Independent on Sunday

9780552153447